Benjamin Taylor

The World on Wheels

Benjamin Taylor

The World on Wheels

ISBN/EAN: 9783743369122

Manufactured in Europe, USA, Canada, Australia, Japa

Cover: Foto ©Andreas Hilbeck / pixelio.de

Manufactured and distributed by brebook publishing software (www.brebook.com)

Benjamin Taylor

The World on Wheels

THE WORLD ON WHEELS

AND OTHER SKETCHES

BY Benj. F. Taylor

CHICAGO,
S. C. GRIGGS & CO.
1874

PRINTED AT THE LAKESIDE PRESS,

CLARK AND ADAMS STS.,

CHICAGO.

ONLY THIS:

The Wheels in this book ran, during the summer of 1873, through the columns of The New York Examiner and Chronicle, to "the head and front of whose offending," the

REV. EDWARD BRIGHT, D.D.,

who gave those wheels "the right of way," the old rolling stock and a miscellaneous cargo is

Cordially Consigned.

ROLLING STOCK AND BILL OF LADING.

THE WORLD ON WHEELS.

BAGGAGE.

ILLUSTRATIONS.

THE WORLD ON WHEELS.

CHAPTER I.

THE perpetual lever called a wheel is the masterpiece of mechanical skill. At home on sea and land, like the feet of the Proclaiming Angel, it finds a fulcrum wherever it happens to be. It is the alphabet of human ingenuity. You can spell out with the wheel and the lever — and the latter is only a loose spoke of that same wheel — pretty much everything in the Nineteenth Century but the Christian Religion and the Declaration of Independence. Having thought about it a minute more, I am inclined to except the exceptions, and say they translate the one and transport the other.

Were you ever a boy? Never? Well, then, my girl, was n't one of your first ambitions a finger-ring? And there is your wheel, with a small live axle in it! But whatever you are, did you ever know a boy worth naming and owning who did not try to make a wheel out of a shingle, or a board, or a scrap of tin? Maybe it was as eccentric as a comet's orbit, and only *wabbled* when it was meant to whirl, but it was the genuine curvilinear aspiration for all that. Boys, young and old, "take to" wheels as naturally as they take to sin. I am sorry for the fellow that never rigged a water-wheel in the spring swell of the meadow brook, or mounted a wind-mill on the barn gable, or drew a wagon of his own make. My sympathies do not extend to his lack of a velocipede, which is nothing if not a bewitched and besaddled wheelbarrow.

In fact, it seems to be the tendency of everything to *be* a wheel. There's your tumbling dolphin, and there's your whirling world. The conqueror whose hurry set on fire the axles of his chariot was no novelty. Who knows that the Aurora Borealis and the Aurora Australis, lighting up the sky about the polar circles in the night-time, may not be the flashes from the glowing axles of the planet? Who knows that the ice and snow may not be piled up about the Arctic and Antarctic just to keep the flaming gudgeons as cool as possible? Does Sir John Franklin? Does *any*body?

Take an old man's memory. Only give it a touch, and it turns like a wheel between his two childhoods, and 1810 comes round before you can count the spokes, and 1874 hardly out of sight.

When they made narrow wooden hands with slender wrists, and called them oars, and galleys swept the Eastern seas in a grave and stately way, they did well. When they fashioned broad and ghastly palms of canvas that laid hold upon the empty air, and named them sails, they did better. When they grouped around an axle the iron hands that buffeted the waves and put the sea, discomfited, rebuked, behind the flying ship, they had their wheel, and they did best!

A one-horse wagon — for nothing was buggy then, but neglected bedsteads — artistically bilious, and striped like a beetle, with a paneled box high before and behind, like an inverted *chapeau*, and a seat with a baluster back, softened and graced with a buffalo robe, warm in winter — and in summer also — was one of the wheeled wonders of my boyhood. No sitting in that wagon like a right-angled triangle — room in front for any possible length of leg, and a foot-stove withal — room behind for two or three handfuls of children, and a little hair-trunk with a bit of brass-nail alphabet on the cover. Curiously enough, the wagon was owned by that noble Baptist pioneer of the New York North Woods, Elder — not Reverend but revered — JOHN BLODGETT, and in it he used to traverse "East road,"

and " West road," and " Number Three road,"
and go to Denmark and Copenhagen and Leyden
and Turin, and other places in foreign parts,
without shipping a sea, or, to borrow a morsel
of thunder, without " seeing a ship." His was
the voice of " John crying in the wilderness"—
John, the Beloved disciple, he surely was.

Before he went to " the Ohio," for that is
what they called it in the years ago, he preached
a farewell to the saddened friends, " Sorrowing
most of all that they should see his face no
more," and then some Christians, some children
and some sinners accompanied him ten miles on
his way, and, after that, the paneled wagon was
lost in the wilderness and the West, and we all
turned sorrowing home, and his words "no more"
proved true.

And the next wheeled wonder was a calash-
topped chaise, heavy, squeaky on its two great
loops of leather springs, and a swaying, sleepy
way with it, that, for the occupants was as easy
as lying, but for the horse as wearisome as Pil-
grim Christian's knapsack of iniquity.

CHAPTER II.

THE CONCORD COACH.

FIFTY miles north of Utica, New York, as the crow flies, there is a village. What there was of it in the old days lay in the bottom of a bay of land bounded on the north, south, and west by wooded hills, with some stone-mason work in them older than the Vatican. But now the beautiful town rises like a spring-tide high up the green sides of the bay. Once in twenty-four hours over the south hill lurched a stage-coach. The tin horn was whipped out of its sheath by the driver, and a short, sharp, nasal twang rang out, rising sometimes in one long clear note, that warbled away in an acoustic ringlet, like its aristocratic cousin with a mouth like a brazen morning-glory — the bugle.

Every thing in the little village was broad awake. Doors flew open, faces were framed in at the windows, children hung on the gates. Then the driver gathered up the ribbons of his four-in-hand, swung off from the coach-top his

long-lashed whip with its silken cracker, flicked
artistically the off leader's "nigh" ear, gave the
wheelers a neighborly slap, and with jingle of
chains and rattle of bolt, and a sea-going rock
and swing, down the hill he thundered and
through the main street, the horses' ears laid
close to their heads like a running rabbit's, a
great cloud of dust rolling up behind the leather
"boot" the color of an elephant, the passengers
looking out at the stage windows, until, with a
jolt and one sharp summons of the horn, like the
note of a vexed and exasperated bee, the craft
brings-to at the Post-office, and the driver whirls
the padlocked pouch out from under his mighty
boots to the ground, and then exploding the tip-
end of his twelve-foot lash like a pistol-shot, he
makes a sweep and comes about with a rattling
halt in front of the stage-house. The fat old.
landlord — fat and old when you were a boy, and
alive yet — shuffles out in slippers, opens the
coach-door, swings down the little iron ladder
with two rounds, and the passengers make a
landing. One of them may have been General
Brady, the man who said, or so they say, when
told he could not survive the illness that pros-
trated him, "Beat the drum, the knapsack's
slung, and Hugh Brady is ready to march!" Or
it may have been Joseph Bonaparte, ex-king,
and yet with his head on, which is not after

the historic manner of monarchs out of business,
going to his wilderness possessions in the North
Woods.   Or it may have been Frederick Hass-
ler, the Swiss, Chief of the United States Survey
in the long ago, *en route* for Cape Vincent — the
man who knew more and tougher mathematics

THE CONCORD COACH

than all of his successors together, and who
could say more while the hostlers were changing
horses than anybody else could say in sixty
minutes.   Meanwhile the spanking team, loosed
from the coach, file off in a knowing way and
a cloud of steam, meeting with a snort of recog-
nition the relay that is filing out to take their
places.

That yellow, mud-bespattered stage, with " E.

MERRIAM, No. *something*," blazoned on the doors, was the one thing that linked the small village with the great world, brought tidings of wars, accidents and incidents, that had grown gray on the journey, and word from far-away friends whose graves might have waxed green while the letters they had written, and secured with a round red moon of a wafer, and sealed with a thumb or a thimble, were yet trampled beneath the driver's feet like grain on the threshing-floor. Think of that coach creeping like an insect, for sixpence a mile, and five miles to the hour, to and fro between East and West, the only established means of communication! Think of its nine passengers inside, knocked about like the unlucky ivories in a dice-box, between New York and Detroit, between Boston and Washington. They get in, all strangers; the ladies on the back seat, the man who is sea-sick, by one coach-window, the man that chews "the weed, it was the devil sowed the seed," at the other; somebody going to Congress, somebody going for goods, somebody going to be married. They are all packed in at last like sardines, with perhaps an urchin chucked into some crevice, to make all snug. There are ten sorts of feet, and two of a sort, dovetailed in a queer mosaic upon the coach-floor. The door closes with a bang, the driver fires a ringing shot or two from his whiplash, and away they pitch and lurch. Think of them riding all day, all night, all day again, crushed hats and elbowed ribs, jumping up and bouncing down into each other's laps every little while with some plunge of the coach; butting at each other in a belligerent way, now and then, as if " Aries the ram " were the ruling sign for human kind; begging each other's pardon, laughing at each other's mishaps, strangers three hours ago, getting to know each other well and like each other heartily, and parting at last with a clasp of the hand and a sigh of regret. I think a fifty-mile battering in a stage-coach used to shake people out of the shell of their crustaceous proprieties, and make more lifelong friends than a voyage of five thousand miles by rail. The contemplation for a day or two of a woman's back-hair or a man's bumps of combativeness, is about as merry as a catacomb tea-party, and about as conducive to lively friendships.

All of us who have arrived at years of discretion — had Methuselah ? — have had a suspicion for some time that this is not the same world we were born into. Such a looking-over-the-shoulder as the writer has just indulged in brightens the dim suspicion into certainty, It *is* a grander world, with grander needs and· agencies to match. The little iron wheels have trundled

the big wooden wheels out of the way. The
dear old Concord coaches of the past are driven
to the confines of civilization. Jehu has swung
himself down from his box, thrust the butt end
of his whip-stock into the tin horn's mouth, hung
them up on a nail behind the door, and died.
The swallows flash in and out at the diamond
lights in the old stage barn, its only occupants.

I visited Fort Scott a while ago — Fort Scott,
Kansas, that wonderful bit of metropolitan vigor
in the wilderness. The Missouri, Kansas and
Texas Railroad had reached it, and gone on to
the Indian country. It had been a grand center
for radiating stage lines, and the day the stages
were to break up camp at Fort Scott and go
deeper into Kansas, farther into Missouri, somebody, who had caught the sentiment of the
thing, proposed that all the coaches should be
grouped in one place, and a photographer should
train his piece of small artillery upon them, and
so they should be "taken." The picture is
before me. The four-in-hands, the great coaches,
the snug covered hacks for the cross cuts, the
drivers in position, drivers and stages alike "all
full inside," and a sprinkling of deck passengers.
It was the work of an instant; the coaches were
emptied and wheeled away, to be seen and heard
and welcomed and looked after in Fort Scott
no more.

CHAPTER III.

THE RAGING CANAL.

THE world has certainly grown. Putting the
period just in time, the statement is a safe one
—"has certainly grown." When De Witt Clinton developed the Dutch idea in America, and
made a line of poetry from tide-water to Lake
Erie, which people vilified and christened "Clinton's Ditch," the world was not quite ready for
it, and the Governor went ahead in a canal-boat!
Fancy that world distanced by a three-horse-
power tandem team at six miles an hour to-day.

But it was a stately affair then. There was
a barrel of salt water standing at the bow of
the packet-boat. There was the proud and portly
Governor erect behind the barrel like Virgil's
ears of attention — *arrectis auribus.* There were
the horses rosetted and bespangled. There were
the high and mighty dignitaries on deck, clustered like young bees on a hive's front door-step
at swarming time. There were the enthusiastic
crowds along the way. Arrived at Buffalo, amid

surges of music and rattle of cannon, the Chief
Executive poured that brackish Atlantic water
into the fine indigo blue of Lake Erie. It was
was not quite so grand as the old ceremonial
when the Doge of Venice wedded the Adriatic,
but it *meant* a great deal more. It meant Bishop
Berkely, who said something about a Westward-
going star, of which some mention has been made
once or twice. It meant Ohio, Michigan, Illinois, in that far future which is our instant
present. It meant EMPIRE! You can count the
acts that have meant more, within a hundred
years, upon four fingers and a thumb—more than
ladling out that barrel of sea-water in a strange
place. Well, the boats began to slide along the
thoroughfare of water, and go up stairs and down
stairs in a strange way; and they multiplied like
the sluggard's schoolma'am,—who was his *ant*,
also,—till there are boats in sight in summer
days everywhere between Buffalo and tide-water;
and they grow larger, till there are a thousand
craft on the Erie Canal of greater tonnage than
the vessel from whose deck Lawrence sent up the
dying charge that made him as deathless as the
Pleiades.

The cargoes of those boats, when they began
to creep, was something wonderful: men, women
and children; plows, axes and Bibles; teachers,
preachers and Ramage presses, along with bed-

steads that corded up and creaked like gates in high winds; big wheels, little wheels and reels, looms with timber enough in them for saw-mills and a log or two left to begin upon. So you see, when they went West in those days they packed up their homes and took them along. You were sure of their finding anchor-ground somewhere, for how could a man go adrift with a wife, five children, a brass kettle and a feather-bed tied to him? You were sure, too, that the world would not be wronged out of a home — perhaps a better and a happier one than the man set afloat on Clinton's Ditch for a place nearer sundown.

Thus it was that the grand westward drift of things received its first impulse. Churches with steeples to them, school-houses full of children, newspapers, farms, Christian homes, not one of which appeared on the bills of lading, were all tumbled aboard the canal-boat amidships or somewhere, though nobody seemed to know it. The mighty fleet of white-decked " liners," looking like Brobdignagian — that word won't hurt you if you do n't go near it ! — ants' eggs with windows in them, has had more to do with the march of civilization than all the aquatic armaments that ever thundered. Sometimes, scurrying along in the cars at thirty miles an hour, you catch glimpses of nests of these eggs adrift in the green fields,

4

floating by the white villages, and advancing, by
contrast, so wonderfully slow that they go backward. Now and then a chit of a girl, with a
little market-basket of garden vegetables upside
down on the top of her head, or a young fellow
who parts his hair in the middle, and has nothing
else to part with worth mentioning, catches a
glimpse of the eggs, too, and tosses a sniff of
contempt at them out of the window, never
dreaming that he looks upon a letter or two of
the alphabet of progress.

I never see one of those boats without a sigh
of regret, not· because I want to be captain or
cook or anything, but because I took my first
foreign voyage on one of them, and the boat was
a "liner" at that! We "took ship" at Oneida,
took water along the way, took soundings when
we ran aground, took steamer at Buffalo. It was
a taking trip. Of the passengers, one turned into
Doctor of Divinity, another into Professor of Latin
in the University of Michigan, a third into President of a Southern College, a fourth into the
pastor of a Michigan church, two bright and
pleasant young ladies into dust long ago, and the
seventh and youngest into the writer of this
sketch.

It was a merry, care - free party. Not one of
the survivors can say that for himself to - day.
We were clustered in the little forward cabin.

We ran over the deck to the after-cabin for meals. We sat upon our baggage, and took something more than a bird's-eye view of the country. We told stories and sang songs and dreamed dreams. We went into cool locks where the water splashed and tumbled about the bows, and were glad. We suffocated ourselves with blankets when we crossed the Montezuma mosquitoes. Why not? Verily, there is but one Marsh there, but of mosquitoes there are several. I have heard of Montezuma's death, It was some time ago, but it would have been no wonder had he died young, not because of the love of the Gods, but of the mosquitoes. We sat on the deck and watched the steersman's intonations. When he cried, "Low *bridge!*" we merely ducked our heads; but when he said, "*Low* bridge!" down we went flat upon the floor like a parcel of undiscovered idolaters. The Palinurus slued the stern of the boat around, and we leaped off upon the "heel-path" and took a stroll. He drove bows on upon the opposite shore, and we took a walk on the "tow-path" with the "drive," who looked like a bundle of old clothes, was as smart as a whip, and profane as "our army in Flanders." He sang songs through the night and the rain as happy as a frog, and when, covered with mud and water, he came aboard to eat, he looked like a bewildered muskrat, and his tracks like a muskrat's also.

We used to hear one genuine word of old English in those seafaring days. Perhaps some other
ambitious "liner" was pulling out ahead of us.
You confer with the "drive" as to the chance
of passing it. You offer him a shilling to try,
and his under jaw drops like the lower half of
a bellows. But promise him a "scale"—scale,
skilling, shilling—and he gets all the tough pull
out of his tandem that there is in it, and goes
by if he can. Websterian "probabilities" says
that is not the derivation of "scale" at all, but
no matter. So you see, we went to sea without
leaving shore. Now and then a cigar-shaped
packet, fuller of windows on the sides than ever
a German flute was of finger-holes, would pass
us with a swash and the blast of a bugle to
"open lock," and the three horses at a swinging
trot, the deck crowded with passengers, and the
cook in the kitchen stewing and frying and
roasting himself and the dinner in the same
kettles.

It was the aristocrat of canal craft, the packet
was, the captain was *somebody*, and wore gloves,
and when on my voyage I saw one coming, I
went down into the cabin, red as to my ears,
for something I had forgotten, and that I never
found in time to come out of the egg till the
packet had gone by. It has since occurred to
me that possibly the redness of ears at that

time might not have been a quality so remarkable as their length. How you would like the
snuggery of the cabin now, and the shelf of a
berth that you couldn't turn over in if a heavy
fellow happened to be sagging on the shelf above
you, and the canal-banks even with the top of
your head when you sit down, and the sun about
as hot upon the roof as if he had actually taken
a deck passage and come bodily aboard, is not
a matter of doubt. But the memory of that
voyage is pleasant, after all — after all *what?* all
these years; like the music of Caryl, "pleasant
but mournful to the soul." And should this short
story of a long voyage bring back to any reader
some such journey that *he* took in the years that
are gone, some cheerful hours he spent, some
cherished friends he made, some faces he learned
to love, that for him shall never be changed nor
sent away, then these paragraphs are not vain.

CHAPTER IV.

THE IRON AGE.

THEY tarried longer by the way in those days, and they *lived* longer, most of them. I think, too, they knew each other better, possibly loved each other more, when they went six miles an hour, than we know each other now that we go sixty. Mind, I would have nobody turn into muriate of soda and make a Lot's wife of himself on my account, but then a harness with neither hold-back nor breeching is a dangerous thing unless the world is a dead level, than which nothing is so very dead, not even a grave-yard. The world has certainly grown. These sketches are written at a place in the State of New York known on the old maps as Chadwick's Bay. It is flanked by one of the loveliest villages in all the empire. To that village came the late Rev. Dr. ELISHA TUCKER, whose memory is yet fragrant in the churches—then neither Reverend nor Doctor, but the plain and primitive Elder Tucker—came with his young wife, who went a thousand miles alone, a while ago, to visit friends!—came from Buffalo forty miles along the Lake shore to that lovely village in a one-horse wagon, and took up his life work. There was not a Baptist church west of him. He preached the first sermon anybody ever heard in Cleveland. A schooner with rusty sails came sliding into Chadwick's Bay with his small store of household wealth. The painted Senecas and the smoky Onondagas went gliding about like vanishing shadows. Deer trooped across the landscapes like flocks of sheep. Speckled trout— nature's great piscatorial triumph, if they *did n't* weigh but a pound apiece—spotted with carmine and gold, leaped out of the cold brooks into the sunshine. There is a roll of dull thunder day and night within ear-shot of where I write these lines at Chadwick's Bay. Twenty-five hundred cars rumble by every twenty-four hours. Flocks and herds from a thousand hills and plains roll along on iron casters like pieces ot heavy cabinet- work. Broad harvests trundle Eastward to tide- water. They rattle over the lines of longitude, and set them together in their flight like the stripes on the American flag.

It is the World on Wheels.

The story of the Locomotive is the history of mechanical invention. It is, if you please, the *monogram* of the right-hand cunning of mankind.

In its finished state, standing upon the track as it does to-day, in its burnished bravery of steel and brass, its shining arms thrust into the caskets slung lightly at its sides, ready at an instant's notice to pluck out great handfuls of power and toss them in fleecy volumes along the way — I want Job to take a look and tell us all about it. He that so described a horse of flesh and blood that Landseer could have painted the creature if he had never seen one, must be able to handle the Locomotive without gloves. Job would have been the man for the job.

Did you ever tell anybody that the Locomotive is a familiar acquaintance of yours — that you are on speaking terms with it? If you never did, then never do, for it will strain your listener's credulity and your credibility fearfully. I have a sort of touch-the-brim-of-the-hat respect for the thing, and am never so busy that I cannot give it a civil look as it goes by. The dull prose strikes into a quickstep as I think about it:

Would ye know the grand Song that shall sing out the age —
That shall flow down the world as the lines down the page —
That shall break through the zones like a North and South river
From winter to spring making music forever?
I heard its first tones by an old-fashioned hearth,
'T was an anthem's faint cry on the brink of its birth!
'T was the tea-kettle's drowsy and droning refrain,
As it sang through its nose as it swung from the crane. .

T was a being begun and awaiting its brains —
To be saddled and bridled and given the reins.
Now its lungs are of steel and its breathings of fire,
And it craunches the miles with an iron desire,
Its white cloud of a mane like a banner unfurled,
It howls through the hills and it pants round the world!
It furrows the forest and lashes the flood,
And hovers the miles like a partridge's brood.

Oh! stand ye to-day in the door of the heart,
With its nerve raveled out floating free on the air,
And *feeling* its way with ethereal art
By the flash of the Telegraph everywhere,
And then think, if you can, of a mission more grand
Than a mission to LIVE in this time and this land;
Round the World for a sweetheart an arm you can wind,
And your lips to the ear of listening Mankind!

There used to be a question and answer in the
old manuals of Chemistry that shut together like a
pair of scissors: "What are the precious metals?
Gold and silver." How will it do to amend and
let the mouthful of catechism run thus: "What
are the precious metals? Iron and brass." Iron
for wheels, and brass for people! That is better
because it is truer. Whoever is curious to know
how the name of a certain alloy of copper and
zinc came to take in a mental and moral quality
as a third ingredient, need only post himself a
little in insular literature. The rich ore of the
copper mines of Cyprus was called Cyprian brass.
Venus was the chief divinity of the Cyprian people's adoration. Queerly enough, their quality

struck into their *mines* like a thunderbolt, and the name of the hard, glittering, resounding metal came to have a meaning that could not possibly pertain to a well-behaved pair of brass andirons. Brass in the face is a good thing in a wrong place, but besides making a capital bearing for a rail-car axle, a little in a man's purposes, as the world goes, is not so very bad an alloy after all. It may make them *last* longer, if nothing more.

CHAPTER V.

THE IRON HORSE.

THE world had to wait a weary time for its wheels, simply because the successors of Tubal and Jubal took something for granted. It is never safe, as every day's experience proves, to take anything or anybody for granted. The only safety in praising the average man is to hold on to your eulogy till he is dead, and done doing altogether. What the cunning artificers took for granted was this: an engine's pulling power is equal to its own weight. And so they made wheels with teeth, and rails with cogs, to help the thing along. They rigged an anomalous, pre-Adamite fowl's foot with a corrugated sole, on each side of the engine. These feet were set down one after the other upon the roughened rail, and pushed the awkward affair in a sort of dromedary way, monstrous to contemplate and tedious to wait for. Device followed device, all as vain as the achievement of perpetual motion, until some man, after a Columbus fashion when

he played with a hen's egg, said: Is this *true*
that we have all been taking for granted? Will
not an engine 'pull more than its own weight?
Let us try it. *They* did, and *it* did. It trailed
long streets and great towns of cars—which were
warehouses and dwellings and palatial mansions;
which were sheep-folds and cattle-yards and coal
mines — after it at twenty, forty, fifty miles an
hour, as if real estate belonged to the ornitho-
logical kingdom, and had taken perpetual flight
like Logan's cuckoo.

When you see a brace of iron bars laid parallel upon the ground, and a harp of wire strung
along beside it, you see the fragment of a man
that can never indulge in a soul without bor-
rowing one. It is the line of a mighty muscle,
and the thread of a fine nerve. On the one,
thoughts fly—thoughts that are "up and dressed"
in their verbal clothes. On the other, things.
The one is seven-ninths of a Scriptural aspiration five-ninths realized: "O that I had the
wings of a dove, that I might fly away—and
be at rest." The other is the consolidated arm
of Christendom, the common carrier of the mov-
able world. But grand as it is, and priceless as
are the treasures it is bearing, it was too late
for the holiest burden of all time. There was no
train to Jerusalem, and the Lord of Life rode into
the city in the humblest guise, upon a donkey.

At Omaha, one day, I saw a steam caravan
come in from what used to be a "forty years
in the wilderness" region, direct from the Golden
Gate. It was the tea-train from the Celestial
Kingdom. It was nothing to look at — the dingy,
battered cars, the engineer as if he had been
wrestling with a coal-heaver — but it was much
to think of. That cargo came right out of the
West, straight from the "Drowsy East." The
bars of the trans-continental railroad had careened
the horizon with their mighty leverage, and let
the cargo through—the very cargo for which they
waited in the old days with their faces toward
the rising sun, like a praying Israelite. The locomotive had wheeled the rolling globe a half revolution, brought the tide of commerce to the
right-about, like a soldier upon his heel. It has
proved to be anything but what it was suspected of being — the locomotive has — for, made
to be a common carrier, a gigantic, quicktime
dray-horse, it is a civilizer, a builder of cities;
and if the three W's, Messrs. Wesley Brothers
and Whitefield, will forgive me, a sort of—
Methodist; in fact, an outright circuit-rider, and
a missionary, withal! The preachers of flesh and
blood denounced the seraglio and the harems of
the American Desert, but nobody minded it.
The law-makers frowned upon them, and they
grew like a garden of cucumbers; were about

as far beyond their jurisdiction as the household economy of "the man in the moon." The locomotive made for them at last, from Atlantic and Pacific; it brought the Gentiles and the "Saints" shoulder to shoulder; its mountain-eagle elocution rang through the valleys of Utah, and sooner or later it will whistle that barbarism of the Orient down the wind.

The locomotive is a civilizer. It happened to the writer to witness the splendid display of the Missouri State Fair at Kansas City, that young Chicago of the red Missouri. Altogether it was the most admirable display of agricultural products ever seen in the Far West. Than the artistic grouping of apples in vast variety, nothing finer was ever witnessed. They were literally "apples of gold in pictures of silver." Without spot or blemish, better than ever grew in the Garden of Eden, they were all from the orchards of the wilderness. But the most interesting and suggestive department, as having direct reference to the civilizing agency of the locomotive, was one surmounted with the legend, "The Great American Desert."

Not a thing in it that did not come from the once sterile plain or inaccessible mountain region; that was not grown in the very realm set down upon maps hardly twenty years old as a pathless and arid waste; and not a figure pictured

in it, but a bewildered buffalo or a mounted
savage ; that was not made possible by the magic
touch of railroad iron. What a maker of new
and improved maps is the locomotive! That
department was worthy to be the coat-of-arms
of the Angel of Abundance. Above all, were
the antlers of the elk, like the branches of a
blasted tree; and the shaggy head of a buffalo,
curly as the head of the heathen god of wine.
Then there were stalks of corn that would amaze
you, and as full of ears as Mr. Spurgeon's audi-
ences. There were squashes and melons and
pumpkin-pies in "the original package," in whose
case the usual law of limitation had been sus-
pended, and they had grown on without let or
hindrance. Wheat that Illinois would have been
proud of. Minerals of wonderful richness and
beauty. Grapes in clusters of ideal symmetry
and size. Apples as of a fresh and new creation that no blighting bug or worm had yet
found out. Indeed, think of anything you like
best that grows in a garden, and it was there,
all from the Great American Desert. There was
an address to the assembled thousands, but nothing so eloquent as this upon the power of the
locomotive as a cultivator and civilizer. But for
it, the products would never have been here in
Kansas City, nor the producers there in the
wilderness.

Take the Illinois Central Railway; it was to
that splendid State what the rod of Moses was
to the rock in the wilderness. It smote it into
life and luxuriance. Down from Chicago to Cairo,
just as many miles as there are days in a year,
down from Dunleith to that same capital of
modern Egypt, four hundred and fifty-six miles,
it went,—in its time the stateliest railway enterprise in the world. Had you been a passenger on a southward-bound train of that road, say
sixteen years ago, you would have traversed a
region of magnificent possibilities. True, the locomotive would have hurried you through un-
fenced corn-fields nine miles long, whose rows
swung round as the cars flew on, like vast bri-
gades on drill, but you would have struck out,
at last, upon the untilled and almost untrodden
pastures of God. You could never forget it.
The month was September. The train had
reached the center of a grand prairie. The few
passengers debarked, and the train ran on a
half mile and left us alone. Around on every
side, the prairie curved up to the edge of the
sky. It was a mighty bowl, and we, served up
in the bottom of it, a very diminutive bill of
fare for such a tremendous dish. The gaudy
yellow and red Fall flowers ornamented the bowl
like some quaint pattern for Chinese ware. Not
a tree nor a living thing in sight; not a sign

that man had ever been an occupant of the planet, but something that looked like a cigar-box high up the side of the bowl, and was, in fact, a human habitation. The great blue sky was set down exactly upon the edge of the dish, like the cover of a tureen, and there we were, pitifully belittled. The feeling was oppressive. We had nothing small or mean with which to compare ourselves and, *be somebody* again, and were glad to have the train back once more, that we might clamber in and be safe out of the vastness.

On we went till the pleasant little village of Anna was reached. The country was full of peaches. They ripened and fell beside the roads. The swine were fattened upon them. The people had just begun to learn that peaches were money in disguise. The railroad had just taught them this lesson of finance. It had made Chicago, and Union County peaches possible combinations. But they were only beginners, and when you asked a man perched upon a wagon-load of Sunnysides the price, he said, "How many, stranger?" and when you replied, "A couple of dozen," the answer came back like the shutting of a jack-knife blade, "Take 'em along an' welcome!" The locomotive whistled us to quarters, and by-and-by the speed slackened to eight miles an hour. The windows were garnished with heads

in a twinkling. There was a deer on the track,
and bound south, like ourselves. The engineer
crowded him a little, and throwing back his head,
away he went over ties and culverts and little
bridges, the cow-catcher turned into a deer-catcher
for the moment. Again the engineer would let
up a little to give the fellow a chance, and so
for miles, till at last, as if he had wings to his
heels, he bolted the track, bounded over a little
knoll and was gone.

Now, find that big bowl of ours if you can!
Farms checker the prairie. Villages dot the
broad landscape like flocks of sheep. Cities with
mayors to them have sprung up. The locomotive brought the builders, brought the buildings.
In a word, the motive was the *loco*motive. Take
the Chicago & Northwestern Railway across the
States of Illinois and Iowa, across the Rock and
the Mississippi to the banks of the Missouri, four
hundred and eighty-eight miles to Council Bluffs.
Seven years ago its western terminus was New
Jefferson, Iowa. There you took private conveyance for a journey of one hundred and eighty
miles to the Missouri. You launched out over
the great swells of prairie, rising and falling, rising
and falling, till you almost caught yourself listening for the wash of the heavy sea. Little
hamlets at long intervals showed like unnamed
islets. The wolf looked after you as you passed.

The hawks sat in rows on the telegraph wire over which, that minute, a message was flashing to California, the little hawks all facing us with their aquiline countenances, like so many young Romans. The tall prairie grass waved desolately in the wind. The prairie poultry disputed the right of way with the advancing horses. The quick tick of the locusts, all winding their watches at once, sounded loud and clear in the silence. Dismantled stage barns roofed with prairie hay were sparsely sprinkled along the route. At last we struck out upon a thirty-mile stretch without a human habitation. The clouds and the sun played tricks with the landscape. Now you thought you saw a field of red wheat ripe for the sickle, and now a scraggy old orchard dwarfed in the distance. The one was a family of little oaks, the other the long tawny grass of the prairie slopes.

It was a virgin world. You had escaped from the clank of engines and the clamor of men. The air swept by without a taint of smoke or any human naughtiness. Your pulse played with an evener beat. You were not quite sure you ever wanted to get out of the wilderness at all. You meet now and then a " freighter," as the ox-expressmen of plain and prairie are called, with their noisy tongues and explosive whips, and their four, six, eight yokes of lumbering oxen trailing

a yet more lumbering wagon.   Then you come
to Ida Grove, with a hospitable tavern in it.
Then fifty miles down the Maple Valley, as un-
peopled and peaceful as the Happy Valley of
Rasselas.   Seven years ago!   And now it is farms
and houses and villages all the way.   Churches
point their slender white fingers towards the sky.
School-houses hum with the busy tongues of the
disciples of "b, a, ba, k, e, r, ker, baker."   Railway trains go scurrying along.   The locomotive
has brought the world to the wilderness, and took
back for "return freight" the wilderness to the
world.   The old trick of the clouds and the sunshine has been played again.   There *are* sweeps
of ripened grain upon the slopes.   There *are*
orchards that are not oaks.

CHAPTER VI.

PLUNGING INTO THE WILDERNESS.

Th&y have discovered that our next-door neighbor, the moon, is about the temperature of boiling water. What a splendid locomotive was spoiled just to make a moon! Those of us who are forty years old have been spending the last twenty in unlearning much they had persuaded us to believe in the first ten. No Great African Desert. No Great American Desert. No giants in Patagonia, except little ones. No William Tell, no apple, no target practice. "G. Washington" never had a hatchet. No Maelstrom off the Norwegian coast. No White Nile mystery. Homer never wrote Homer, nor Ossian Ossian. There are two things, two blessed doubts, that we know as little about as we ever did, to-wit: Who wrote the Letters of Junius? and Is there an open Polar Sea? I sincerely hope they will never find out.

The locomotive is aggressive. It assaults and captures and tames the wilderness. You are a passenger on the Missouri, Kansas and Texas Railway, that can swing you down through Missouri and the Indian Territory and Texas to the Gulf of Mexico. You embark at Sedalia, the most vigorous inland town in Missouri except Kansas City. The cars are as elegant as any in America, the track smooth to a wonder, and altogether the perfection of locomotive civilization. Away you glide. Fort Scott is passed, and the train begins to show queer characteristics. The men that get aboard are leaner and longer, with a swinging stride like so many panthers. They carry brown rifles, they are girt about with a small armament of revolvers. They are in full blossom as to the brims of their hats, like sunflowers. They talk deer, horse, bear, turkey. They brevet you, and you become captain or colonel by the breath of their mouths, which is tobacco. There are sleepy-looking dogs in the baggage-car, with ears like little leather aprons. You see more flat women in sunbonnets than you ever saw before in one place. Three or four exaggerated creatures lie in a heap in a corner. They are the half-way station between a large rabbit and a small donkey. They are ears with bodies to them. It is your first sight of a buck-rabbit. You hear border talk and see border manners, in cars finished to the last touch of pier-glass polish. You look up, and lo, a Cherokee at your elbow! There he stands, as if a fresh creation, and positively his first appearance anywhere. His eyes, like black beads suddenly struck with intelligence, had taken you all in before you saw him at all. You begin to realize where you are —that old Fort Holmes is at your right and Little Rock at your left; that you are in a country with such places in it as Elk City, Panther, Yéllville, Crockett and Waxahatchie.

Again, you are on the Atchison, Topeka and Santa Fé Railway. You land at Emporia, Kansas, one hundred and twenty-eight miles from Kansas City. The locomotive breasts the prairie in panoply as glittering as anywhere. You find a brisk and busy town, well-filled stores, elegant houses, capital schools, a public library, and intelligent and hospitable people. The railroad was Pharaoh's daughter to it. It found the little Moses in the bulrushes, and made Emporia a marvel in the wilderness. You see last week's New York fashions in the streets, the latest works of literature upon the tables. The pretty dining-room girl startles your left ear at breakfast with, "Buffalo-steak or antelope?" You regard her in a dazed way, and ask "What?" "Buffalo - steak or antelope?" and you say "*Both!*" A citizen, on hospitable thoughts intent, promises to take you out antelope - hunting. You faintly enquire "Where?" and the reply is, "O, ten or a dozen

miles!" You begin to understand things, and to
see that the locomotive is trailing civilization
along after it wherever it goes.

Again on the train: A man enters the car who
toes straight out the way he is going. He has a red
sash, silk, and Chinese at that, about his waist.
The glitter of a silver-mounted revolver at his
left side, a shady sombrero upon his head, an un-
civilized nugget of gold for a breastpin, a small
log-chain of the same material a-swing upon his
breast, buttons up and down the side seams of
his pantaloons, square-shouldered, broader at the
breast than equatorially. There you have him,
and *is n't* he cool? He gives you a square look
with both eyes. He seats himself upon the crimson cushions as indifferently as if he had never
seen anything else. It is an American turned
into a Mexican herder, arrayed in his holiday
clothes, and bound for St. Louis. He is at home
on horseback, is at home *any*where, and can
throw a lariat like a savage. He takes an apple
out of one pocket, a desperate-looking knife out
of another; a little jerk of the wrist, and about
eight inches of steel blade flash out, he looks at
you a second, and—carves his apple! Then that
cutlery becomes a toothpick of the Arkansas
patent. He will tell you it is a frog-sticker.

I should like to see the railroad-hog, a variety
in the animal kingdom of which there is some-

thing to be said by-and-by, get his seat while he is in the baggage-car taking a smoke. If carved ox is beef, and manufactured calf is veal, that hog would be in danger of turning into pork. Though the herder is quiet, civil, self-reliant, yet he is a peripatetic Bill of Rights. He is his own Legislature, and the first law is self-defence. He answers your questions in a quaint, sententious way. He will tell you that a great herd of those Southwestern cattle look like a drove of horns with legs and tails to them; that they all think a man has four feet, and is half horse. They seldom see him except mounted, and when they do, that man must make "a right smart" use of the two feet he has left, to escape being gored and trampled to death. Those illogical cattle have no idea of the concrete. The herder loves the free life, the swift motion, the abundant air, and the elbow-room of the plains. He has not taken as much medicine as you can put on a knife-blade in eight years. When he is "under the weather," he just curls down somewhere, and sleeps it off like a dog.

Yonder are a couple of rough men, with North-easterly voices, and shaggy about the head as a couple of buffaloes. They have just come in from killing two hundred of those "cattle upon a thousand hills." They *think* they are hunters. They are unacquainted with Webster, and miss the right word, for they are unlicensed *butchers*, and ought to be punished. They had slain the two hundred for their tongues alone, and left the great carcasses a reckless waste upon the plains. If those fellows could only have an Egyptian "lean year" all to themselves, I should like to put them on a strictly vegetable diet, and turn them out to graze with Nebuchadnezzar. Such touches of border-life give a Far Western train a character of its own that is by no means unpleasant. You feel something as you did when you entered the National Conservatory at Washington, breathed the scented air of the home-made tropic and saw the great-leafed palms, and waited a minute for an elephant to come out.

But let nobody think that the world on wheels in Kansas, Nebraska, Texas and the Plains essentially differs from the same world trundling about in New England. Equal courtesy, heartier cordiality, just as much intelligence as characterize the route from New York to Boston. Writing of Boston: A certain publishing house in that city once sent a letter to a Chicago citizen, and a man to bring it, asking for a list of those places in the West where the people would be "*up* to their publications," for that is the way they put it. The Chicago citizen referred them to a great fat Gazetteer, and the inquisition ended.

CHAPTER VII.

VICIOUS ANIMALS.

A great many animals get on board first-class passenger trains that should have been shipped in box-cars, with sliding doors on the sides. There is your Railway Hog—the man who takes two seats, turns them *vis-a-vis*, and makes a letter X of himself, so as to keep them all. Meanwhile, women, old enough to be his mother, pass feebly along the crowded car, vainly seeking a seat, but he gives a threatening grunt, and they timidly look the other way. He is generally rotund as to voice and person, well-fed, but not well-bred. Not always, however. I have seen a meek-faced man, as thin and pale as an ivory paper-cutter, who looked as if he had just gone with the consumption, who made an X of *him*self as if he were the displayed emblem of porcine starvation. Have you ever thought of taking up burglary for a livelihood? Be a burglar if you must, but a Railway Hog never! Had the ancestors of this type of creature only been among the herd that ran down that "steep place into the sea," what a comfort it would have been!

Did you ever see the Bouncers? They are young, they are girls, they always go in pairs, and they bring a breeze. Like the man whose voice in secret prayer could be heard throughout the neighborhood, they discuss private affairs in a public manner. They throw scraps of loud, laughing talk at you much as if they were eating a luncheon. It is November. The wind comes out of the keen North. Be-shawled, be-cloaked, be-furred, never laying off fur or feather, they open the windows with a bounce, and there they sit snug as Russian bears, and the wind blowing full upon you seated just behind. You venture to beg, after freezing through, that they will close the windows and let you come to a thaw. What a word "supercilious" is, to be sure! Up go their two pairs of eyebrows, and down come the windows, both with a bounce. Then they grow sultry, and one whisks off "a cloud" or something square in your eyes, and the other flings back her fur cape on to the top of your head, sees what she has done, brushes the garment a little, and says nothing—to you. The train halts at some station. Up go the windows and out the two heads, and a rattling fire of talk is exchanged with more Bouncers on the platform — all loud, talk and talkers, as a scarlet vest and a saffron neck-tie. By-and-by they fall to fixing their back-hair, smoothing their eyebrows with a licked finger, and making other preparations to leave the poor company they have managed to get into.

Lest they be forgotten, let me impound certain offending people in a few paragraphs just here, that, like that place in the Valley of Hinnom, shall be a sort of Railway Travelers' Tophet. Capital punishment should not be abolished until they have all been executed at least *once:*

The man whose salivary glands are the most active part of him, who spits on your side of the aisle when you are not looking, and spoils the lady's dress who occupies the seat after him.

The man who puts a pair of feet, guiltless of water as a dromedary's, upon the back of your seat, and wants you to beg his pardon for·being so near them.

The man who eats Switzer cheese, onions and sausages from over the sea, in the night time.

The man who prowls from car to car, and leaves the doors wide open in the winter time.

The boy who pulls the distracted accordeon by the tail, he having several mothers and six small sisters to feed, and then wishes you to pay him something for " cruelty to animals."

The boy who throws prize packages of impo-

sition at you, and insists you shall buy the
" Banditti of the Prairie," or the " Life of Ellen
Jewett," or the pictorial edition of the Walworth
Family, or a needlebook, or a bag of popped
corn, or some vegetable ivory, and wakes you
out of a pleasant doze to see if you would n't
like a Railroad guide.

The man who, with a metallic voice, in which
brass is as plain as a brass knuckle, does the
wit for the car; who tells the train-boy he'll
get his growth before the train gets through;
who talks of stepping off to pick whortleberries,
and then stepping on again; who says that
orders have been issued to the engineer never
to heat the water hot enough to scald anybody;
who talks in the night, and makes it hideous.
There is no apparent reason why this man may
not be made shorter by a head immediately.
Let him be guillotined. "Brevity is the soul of
wit."

What shall we do with her? — the woman who
sails through the crowded car, and brings to
beside you like a monument, looks as if you had
no business to be born without her consent, and
says in a clear, incisive voice, that cuts you like
a knife, "I know a gentleman when I see him!"
Is there a needle or something in the cushion?
You are seventy, and have the rheumatism. She
is twenty-five, full of strength and health, and

with a pair of supporters of her own as sturdy as the legs of a piano. But what can you do? You feel red, and draw your head into your coat-collar like a modest and retiring mud-turtle, and pretend not to hear. But there she stands, and a young fellow across the way with a sky-blue necktie just lighted under his chin, laughs out loud at the situation, and you think, as pretty much all the blood you have, has gone into your head and ears, you will go and warm your feet. So you get up, with joints creaking like a gate, and hobble to the stove, where you stand and bow to the stove-pipe in an extraordinary way, and catch it around the waist now and then, and all the while she sits in your place like a fallen angel. "What shall we do with her?" Send her to the tailor to be measured, and "let her pass for a man!"

Everybody has met the man on a railway train who, as no one ever learned his name because no one ever cared to, may be designated as "*Might I?*" with a rising slide. All sorts of a man to look at, he is but one sort of a man to encounter, to-wit: an animated cork-screw, forever trying to pull the cork from the bottle of your personal identity. "Might I?" begins his acquaintance by *stealing;* stealing a look at you out of the tail of his eye, the meanest kind of pilfering, though the law does n't mention it.

Then he begins upon you. He says, " Might I ask how far you are traveling ? Might I inquire what business you follow ? Might I inquire if you are married ? Might I ask your name ? " His talk is as lively as a mite-y cheese, and he assaults you like the New England Catechism. This man has been growled at, snapped at, requested to go beyond the possible limit of frost, but he cuts and comes again the very first opportunity. " Might I?" has never been put to death by anybody. The remedy could be tried once, and if it failed to quiet, and only killed him, we should know better than to try it again.

The Railway Opossum is not vicious but he is amusing. He enters a car that is rapidly filling, drops into a whole seat, adjusts his blanket, chucks his soft hat under his head, swings up his feet to a horizontal — all this in two minutes — and is asleep ! Objurgations fall upon him like the sweet rain. Shakes fail to disturb him, and no one ever tried Shakespeare. Tender women passing by say, " O, he 's asleep — perhaps worn out with long travel; " and not till that swarm settles, and he thinks himself sure of his elbow-room, does he open an eye and " come to," and grow as lively as opossums ever get.

They board the train — they two — he in white gloves, new clothes, and a white satin necktie; she in a lavender silk, a bridal hat, and a small blush. Seated, they incline towards each other like the slanting side-pieces of the letter A. He throws one arm around her, and she reclines on his shoulder like a lily-pad. They whisper, they giggle, they talk low, they contemplate each other like a couple of china cats on a mantle-piece. He takes a gentle pinch of her cheek as if she were maccaboy, when she is only a very verdant girl. She sits with her hand in his, like a mourner at a funeral — the funeral of propriety. They punctuate their twitter of talk with pouncing kisses. They fly at each other like a brace of humming-birds. The sun shines. The car is filled with strangers. They are the target for thirty pairs of eyes. They smell of cologne or patchouly or — musquashes! They are the sorghum of the honeymoon — saccharine lunatics, and there they are — turned loose upon the public!

The Union Pacific Company has made provision to shut such people up. They have just begun to run a lunatic asylum with every San Francisco train, but they give it an astronomical name. They call it a "honeymoon car." The Company deserves well of the public for keeping traveling idiots out of sight. In certain circumstances it *is* difficult for some people to avoid being fools.

The ? that wears clothes, and goes away from home by the cars, and afflicts the conductor and

8

the brakeman and his traveling companions — he is of recent origin. There is no account of him in Job. The Patriarch had a great many uncomfortable things, but he did n't have *him.* Had he been let loose upon Pharaoh, that stiff-necked Egyptian would have "let the people go" before breakfast. His natural diet is conductors and brakemen, but he will not refuse anybody. He has told the man before him and the woman behind him where he wants to go, and shown his ticket and his trunk check, and asked if this is the right train, and if the check is good, and when he will get there, and how far it is, and whether he knows anybody there. His victim pronounces the check genuine, gets out his "Guide," hunts up the place, ascertains the distance, tells him the time, and *does n't* know anybody there.

The conductor enters, collecting tickets and fare, has a heavy train, and it is only five miles to the first station. ? makes for him on sight, tries to get him by the collar or button or elbow, and tells him where he wants to go, and shows his check, and inquires if this is the right train, and when he will get there, and how far it is. The conductor answers him, nips a spiteful nick out of his ticket, and hurries on. ? returns to his seat, and watches for a brakeman. Him he catches by the coat-tail, and he asks him if he is on the right train, and if the check is good, and if he thinks his baggage is aboard, and when he will get there, and how far it is. The brakeman has seen him before, and his replies are too short for a weak stomach, but he tells him.

The last morsel finished, he turns to you, and he says, as a woman who deliberates and is therefore lost, " I think now I am on the wrong train. I thought so all the while," and then he tells you where he wants to go, and shows you his check, and asks you if you think. it is good for the trunk, and how far it is, and when he will get there, and you tell him. The conductor returns, he makes a grab at him, and he wants him to tell him when he will get there, and who keeps the best house, and how far it is from the depot, and whether that is really the best house or some other, and whether he meant three o'clock in the forenoon or afternoon, and the conductor does n't tell him.

CHAPTER VIII.

HABITS OF ENGINES AND TRAIN MEN.

A locomotive has two habits. It drinks and it smokes. It seems to take comfort in drinking at a liberal river, rather than where the draught is trickled out to it through a stingy pipe on a dry prairie. Climbing heavy grades involves hard drinking. On the Mount Washington Railway, where you travel a mile and rise nineteen hundred feet in an hour and half, the thirsty engine disposes of eighteen hundred gallons of water — all dissipated in breath.

During the late war they often watered engines from pails, as they would ponies. Perhaps you have sat upon a bank, not of thyme but of time, at midnight, in Tennessee, with suspicious cedars all about within *hailing* distance — trees that often shed queer fruit in a vigorous way — waiting for the train-men to bring locomotive refreshments of light wood and pails of water. Never since then has the smoke of an engine been welcome, but often, in those times when the nights were "unruly," would the burning red cedar load the air with a suspicion of sweet incense that was really grateful. Possibly it was associated with the perfume of the cedar bows of boyhood, when the flight of one's own arrow, sped from the springing wood, was grander than any flight of eloquence the archer has heard since. To-day, a whiff of cedar will carry you faster and farther than a swift engine. It will take almost any half-century-old boy back to the era of blue-striped trousers and roundabouts, and girls with white pantalettes gathered at the bottom; to the time when bow and arrow, windmill and kite, jack-knife, fishhooks and tops, " two old cat," Saturday afternoons and training-days were so many letters in the alphabet of happiness, and he will not be a bit worse for the trip, but younger, gentler and more human.

Writing of boys: till the writer was sixteen years old he never saw a deacon, that he couldn't tell him as quick as he could a squirrel. Sometimes they were tall and thin, but often stout, and as the papers have it, "*prominent* members of society"—measured from the second vest button to the small of the back! But they were always gray, and sometimes venerable. He used to wonder if they were born old, and the idea of a *young* deacon was impossible. The locomotive has hurried up these useful servants of the church, so that they are sometimes picked before they are quite ripe, and sent forward by an early train.

Take a sleek, dark-haired, flare-vested, civet-scented, slim-waisted man in a cut-away, and switching his patent-leathers with a ratan, and you have a deacon that would puzzle Wilderness John, as Agassiz never was puzzled by a new specimen of natural history. But he may be a capital deacon for all that, only in disguise.

The more you travel, the less you carry. The novice begins with two trunks, a valise, a hat-box and an umbrella. He jingles with checks. He haunts the baggage-car like a "perturbed spirit." He ends with a small knapsack, an over-coat and a linen duster. Bosom, collar, wrist-bands, he does himself up in paper like a curl. He is as clean round the edges as the margins of a new book.

We throw away a great deal of baggage on the life journey that we cannot well spare; a young heart, bright recollections of childhood, friends of the years that are gone. And so we "fly light," but we do not fly well.

Let us approach the baggage-man with tender-ness. Let us tender him a quarter, if he in turn will give quarter to our trunk. He is square-built and broad-shouldered. His vigorous exer-cise in throwing things has developed his mus-cles till he projects like a catapult. It is pleas-ant to watch his playful ways, provided you carry your baggage in your hat. He waltzes out a great trunk on its corners till they are as dog-

eared as a school reader. He keeps carpet-bags
in the air like a juggler. While one is going
up another is coming down. Hinges of trunks
give way. There is a smell of camphor and

THE BAGGAGE SMASHER.

paregoric, and a jingle of glass, and a display
of woman's apparel. They are all bundled up
like an armful of fodder, and thrust back into
the offending trunk, and a big word is tumbled
in after them — to keep things down.

Meanwhile, the tremendous voice of the check-

master tolls like a bell, "4689 Cleveland! 271
Rochester!" and the baggage-car is as lively
with all sorts of baggage as corn in a corn-
popper. Things that are marked, "this side up
with care!" come down bottom-side up, like captured mud-turtles. They go end over end, like
acrobats. A rope is stretched around the place of
destruction, to keep the crowd that is watching
the entertainment from being killed. This has
always seemed to me a very touching instance
of the loving kindness of railway officials, and
yet it is possible a spare end of that same rope
might be used in a pleasant way to diversify
the performances about that baggage-car. They
have — I hope he is yet alive — a model baggage-man on the Chicago, Burlington & Quincy
Railroad. He is very feeble. Once he was the
champion ground-tumbler of the West, but now
he has the galloping consumption. He is a melancholy spectacle, but he is a model of his kind.
The baggage moves quietly about him, and yet
the transfer is made rapidly and on time. There
is only one thing that prevents his promotion —
his being made inspector of baggage-men throughout the country, with a commission to travel
and visit them all. It is this: quick consumption is not contagious. Not one of his subor-
dinates could possibly catch it.

Sometimes a train in an accountable way has

a characteristic. Were you ever passenger on the Inarticulate Train? The conductor enters the car, closes the door with a confused bang, and, his little tongs swinging on a finger in an airy way, he shouts "Tix!" The train-boy coasts along behind him, and he says, "Ap! Pape! Norangz!" The brakeman pops his head in at the door, shows you the top of his cap, and roars down into his manly bosom, "Tledr!" just as you are pulling into that misplaced Castilian city, in the region where, according to the old song,

"Potatoes they grow small in Maumee!"

The very wheels beneath you trundle along in an indistinct fashion, and the engine has a wheeze instead of a whistle. It is as if the railway dictionary had been run over by the cars a number of times, and there was nothing left for the owners but to serve out the fragments to passengers. The brakeman of a train holds, all things considered, the post of honor, because the post of danger. The locomotive talks to him all day, and, as a rule, that is about the only individual with whom he holds much conversation. It says "Hold her!" and round goes the wheel. "Danger!" and he springs to it with a will. "Ease her!" and off comes the brake with a clank. "Now I'm going to start!"

"Now I'm going to back!" "Off the track!
Off the track!" "Coming to bridge!" "I see
the town!" "Open the s-w-i-t-c-h!" and,
through all, the brakeman stands by like a helms-
man in a storm. On lightning trains he is not
given to much humor, but the article is in him.
As you cross Iowa by the Chicago and Northwestern Railway, and approach the great Divide,
the stations run: East Side — Tip-Top — West
Side. The route through that region is a little
monotonous. It is the hammer, hammer, hammer
of the wheels in anvil cadence hour after hour.
Between cat-naps, small enough to be kittens, you
see the great swells of prairie, and then more
prairie. But there is a brakeman on one of the
trains that can enliven you a little, and always
brings up a smile like a glimmer of sunshine. He
says "East Side!" or "West Side!" stupidly
enough, but when the train is just halting at the
pinnacle, he throws a hearty elation and a double
circumflex into his tone, much as if you had
asked him what sort of time he had at the great
Railroad Ball, and he cries "Tip-Top!" That
inflection of his always tells.

There is a poor joke, past the grace of saltpetre, that an economical conductor will save a
few hundred dollars a year more than his salary; and there is an impression abroad in many
minds that conductors take to stealing as Dog-

berry got his reading and writing — naturally. When it comes to that, a couple of railway directors and a president or two have been known to steal more money than all the conductors in the United States together *ever* misappropriated. A conductor, if dishonest, is not a rogue because he is a conductor, or a conductor because he is a rogue. As a class, conductors are as honorable as lawyers, physicians, bankers, while they run far greater risks, and have far more to try their patience, than the money-changers and professional gentlemen just named. Go from Providence to the Golden Gate, and, as a rule, it is the conductors who treat you with the most courtesy and kindness, step aside from the line of their official duty to gratify your reasonable wishes and render you comfortable. And not for you only, but for the hundreds of thousands of strangers who ride upon their trains.

To them, generations of men and women only live from eighteen to twenty-four hours. They pass on, and are seen no more. But during those hours the conductor has human nature under a microscope. He discovers things about people that they themselves had only guessed at. He discerns traits that their neighbors never detected. The average conductor is a shrewd man. He reads faces like a book, and remembers them always.

CHAPTER IX.

IN THE SADDLE.

THE engineer and the brakeman are as often
and as truly heroes as the average veteran army
colonel under fire for the tenth time. True courage, thoughtful kindness, presence of mind, and a
quiet bearing, form a four-stranded quality that is
never quite perfect if unraveled. How have they
all been illustrated! Take the hero of New-
Hamburg, on the Hudson River Road, who looked
death in the face, and never left the saddle.
Take the dying engineer immortalized by the poet
of Amesbury, who used the last of his ebbing
breath to make sure the coming train was sig-
nalled. Take incidents chinked into the papers
every day in little type, that, pertaining to men
without shoulder-straps or title, are read with a
passing glance, and then forgotten.

The locomotive engineer is as quiet as a Quaker meeting. One driver of a four-horse coach
will make more noise than a dozen of him.
There he is with his hand upon the iron lever,

and looks forth from his little window. If he wants to say something confidentially to a street crossing, there is the bell-tongue. If he wishes to throw a word or two back to the brakeman, or make a short speech to a distant depot, there is the whistle. He pats his engine, and calls it " she." Its name is Whirling Cloud or Rolling Thunder or Vampire or Vanderbilt, but it is " she" all the time. He knows her ways, and she understands his. He loves to see her brazen trappings shine; to watch the play of her polished arms; to let her out on a straight shoot; to make time.

Put your foot in the stirrup and swing yourself aboard. The engineer's little cabin is a regular houdah for an elephant. It is a princely way of making a royal progress. The engineer bids you take that cushioned seat by the right-hand window. You hear the gurgle of the engine's feverish pulse, and the hiss of a whole community of tea-kettles. There is his steam-clock with its finger on the figure. There is his time - clock. One says, sixty pounds. The other, forty miles an hour. A little bell on the wall before him strikes. That was the conductor. He said " Pull out," and he pulls. The brazen bell, like a goblet wrong side up, spills out a great clangor. The whistle gives two sharp, quick notes. The driver swings back the lever. The engine's slender arms begin to feel slowly in her cylindrical pockets for something they never find, and never tire of feeling for. Great unwashed fleeces are counted slowly out from the smoke-stack. The furnace doors open and shut faster and faster. The faces of the clock dials shine in the bursts of light like newly-washed school-children's that have been polished off with a crash towel. The lever is swung a little farther down. The search for things gets lively. Fleeces are getting plentier. The coal goes into the furnace and out at the chimney like the beat of a great black artery. There is a brisk breeze that makes your hair stream like a comet's.

The locomotive is alive with reserved power. It has a sentient tremor as it hugs the track, and hurls itself along sixty feet for every tick of the clock — as if you should walk twenty paces while your heart beats once! First you get the idea, and next the exhilaration, of power in motion. It is better than "the Sillery soft and creamy," of Longfellow. It is finer than sparkling Catawba. It has the touch of wings in it. You watch the track, and you learn something. You had always supposed the iron bars were laid in two parallel lines. But you see! It is a long slender V, tapering to a point in the distance! But the engine pries them apart as it plunges on, and makes a track of them.

The locomotive quickens your pulse, but it does more. It quickens vegetation, and makes things light and frisky. See that little bush squat to the ground, like a hare in her form. It grows before your eyes. It is a big bush, a little tree, a full-grown maple, that gave down the sap for the sugar-camp kettle in your grandfather's time. There are a couple of portly hay-stacks, like two Dutch burghers of the Knickerbocker days, growing fatter every minute, and waddling out of the way to let the train go by.

Two miles ago, a strolling farm-house stood in the middle of the road, staring stupidly down the track. It has just got over the fence into the lot, behind some shrubs and flowers and pleasant trees, and looks, as you fly by, as if it had never moved at all. Apparently, really, *always*, there is magic in the Locomotive.

There is a picture of the first railroad train in the State of New York. It was taken by a man with no hands. Their proverbial cunning had slipped down into his toes. The faces of the passengers are portraits. One of them is the venerable THURLOW WEED, of New York. The car is strictly a coach. They call a sixty-soul car a coach now. It is a vicious misuse, for a railway-car is as much like a coach as a rope-walk is like a German flute. The vehicle is bodied like a coach, backed like a coach, doored

like a coach, and has a little railing around the
roof to keep the baggage from going overboard.
And there *is* baggage.   It is not a carpet-bag,
nor a valise, nor a Saratoga, but a leather port-
manteau, an Old World cloak-carrier.   There may
be a pair of flapped saddle-bags under somebody's
feet inside.   Modern satchels were not.

There are three seats, and Mr. Weed sits upon
the middle one.   Before this coach is the engine.
The cylinder is trained like a Washington gun,
at an angle of about thirty-three and a third
degrees, and seems to have gotten the range
pretty accurately of the engineer's head.   The
engineer has no house, no seat, but stands upon
a platform much like a man about to be hanged.
A wine-cask, small at both ends and big in the
middle, is perched on end within easy reach,
filled with oven-wood; to-wit, wood split axe-
helve size, such as our fathers were wont to
manufacture for heating the egg-shaped brick
oven on baking days.   With this fuel he pro-
vokes the patient water to boiling point.   No
bell, no whistle, no means of communicating with
him, except the conductor catches him by the
coat-skirt.

The conductor is a "captain."   He has more
dignity than a modern railway superintendent.
They go ten miles an hour, and they do well.
Being in the picture business, I may as well

say that the Harpers once presented a picture
of an old-time iron tea-kettle, with a crooked
spout and a jingling lid. I *saw* it jingle, and
that's direct testimony. From the vexed spout
rolled little volumes of steam. Below it was
the portrait of a great locomotive, all ready to
run. The twain were relatives, for the tea-kettle
was the shriveled, far away, nasal grandfather
of the engine, and beneath it were the words,
"IN THE BEGINNING." That told the story, as
far as the story had gone. These bits of fine art
are suggestive. They mean that we have made
wonderful progress in the art of being common
carriers, and that one-half the world must keep
very busy in thinking things and doing things
worth transporting by the other half. It is an
axiom that no city can achieve permanent pros-
perity simply by an immense carrying trade.
How about the world?

10

CHAPTER X.

RACING AND PLOWING.

Two rates of motion are racing and plowing, but, as you shall see, wonderfully alike. An Agricultural Fair has come to mean a Race-Track with a variety of vegetables ranged around on the outside, and a great crowd between the ring of track and the ring of vegetables. There appears to be much doubt as to the propriety of horse-races, but I have never seen a conscientious man who happened by chance to witness a race, that did not make up his mind in a minute which horse he wanted to be the winner. He did not believe in that kind of four-footed gambling, but then ——. You tell him the gray will be whipped — gray is his color — and he wants to back up his opinion with something — let you know what that judgment is worth to him; and were it not for some restraining grace, he would produce his pocketbook and flourish the estimated value of his opinion full in your face.

That's the way betting comes. It is not a mere invention, like a Yankee nutmeg. It is human nature. One man argues, another sneers, a third gets angry, a fourth fights, and a fifth bets. Five ways of doing the same · thing. The writer knew a young man—not so young as he was—who happened to be in New York when the great running-race between Fashion and Peytona occurred on the Union Course, Long Island. That individual, boy and man, never saw but that one race, never played a game of cards, or bet a penny upon anything; but no sooner were the horses brought up to the Grand Stand than he had his favorite, and he could not have told why, to save his life. He would have endowed that horse's prospect of winning with all his earthly possessions, which were twenty-seven dollars and a half, if he could have found a taker to accept of such a trifle. How he watched every jump the creature made! How he admired her as she flew close to the ground from landing-place to landing-place again, and clapped his hands and cheered like a maniac! He was a full-grown sporting-man in a minute, though he did not know a horse's hock from the Rhenish wine of that name.

Now to put the race upon wheels instead of heels: the tracks of those two great lines of travel, the Michigan Southern and the Pittsburg

& Fort Wayne, run side by side for several miles after they leave Chicago — sometimes so near that you can toss an apple from one train to the other. When the workmen laid the tracks they thought about the races, for they knew that races must come from such a neighborhood of railways, and each gang shouted across to the other, and bet on its own road.

They did come. You are on the Michigan Southern. The train has worked slowly out of the city on to the open prairie. The Pittsburg train has done the same thing. There at your right, and half a mile away, you can see the puffs of white steam. The trembling clangor of the bell has ceased. The shackly-jointed gait of the train ceases. It tightens up, and runs with a humming sound. The landscape slips out from under your feet like a skipping-rope. Pittsburg is coming. She laps the last car of your train. Now is your time to run alongside, and see how an engine acts when the throttle-valve is wide open. Watch the flash of that steel arm as it brings the wheels about. She is doing her best. The two engines are neck and neck. They scream at each other like Camanches. The bells clang. The trains are running forty-five miles an hour. It is a small inspiration.

Now for the passengers. The windows are open. Heads out, handkerchiefs waving. Everybody alive. Everybody anxious. Nobody afraid. Rivalry has run away from fear. Our engineer puts on a little more speed. The train draws slowly out from the even race, like the tube of a telescope. It is the poetry of motion — power spurning the ground without leaving it. Good-by, palaces! good-by, coaches! good-by, baggage-cars! good-by, engine! good-by, *Pittsburg!* We have shown that train a clean pair of heels. There is nothing left of it but black and white plumes of steam and smoke. Look around you. The car is all smiles and congratulations. "Grave and gay," they are as lively as a nest of winning gamblers.

This racing is all wrong. Superintendents have forbidden it, travelers have denounced it, but they want to see what can be gotten out of "Achilles" or "Whirling Thunder," as much as anybody. And they do not want to be beat! Make them engineers, and every man of them would pull out and put things through their best paces. We believe in horses, we believe in locomotives, but we lack faith in balloons. They are large toys for big children. "The earth hath bubbles as the water has, and these are of them."

Old Nantucket salts used to spin their fireside yarns about doubling the Cape. There was such a mingling of peril and excitement; the foamy

seas boarding the ship by the bows; the flying rack; the visible storm; the orders lost in
the thunder of the waves, or swept away by
the wind; it was such man's work to get about
that headland in the Pacific seas, that no wonder boys leaped from bedroom windows in the
night and ran away to try it. I think there is
one railway experience you may have, that is
much like going around the Horn.

Did you ever ride on a snow-plow? Not the
pet and pony of a thing that is attached to the
front of an engine, sometimes, like a pilot, but
a great two-storied monster of strong timbers,
that runs upon wheels of its own, and that boys
run after and stare at, as they would after, and
at, an elephant. You are snow-bound at Buffalo. The Lake Shore Line is piled with drifts
like a surf. Two passenger trains have been
half-buried for twelve hours somewhere in snowy
Chautauqua. The storm howls like a congregation of Arctic bears. But the Superintendent at
Buffalo is determined to release his castaways
and clear the road to Erie. He permits you to
be a passenger on the great snow-plow, and there
it is, all ready to drive. Harnessed behind it is
a tandem team of three engines. It does not
occur to you that you are going to ride upon
a steam-drill, and so you get aboard.

It is a spacious and timbered room, with one

large bull's-eye window — an overgrown lens.
The thing is a sort of Cyclops. There are ropes
and chains and a windlass. There is a bell by
which the engineer of the first engine can signal
the plowman, and a cord whereby the plowman
can talk back. There are two sweeps or arms,
worked by machinery on the sides. You ask
their use, and the Superintendent replies, "when,
in a violent shock, there is danger of the monster's upsetting, an arm is put out on one side
or the other, to keep the thing from turning a
complete somerset." You get one idea, and an
inkling of another. So you take out your Accident Policy for three thousand dollars, and examine it. It never mentions battles nor duels
nor snow-plows. It names "public conveyances."
Is a snow-plow a public conveyance? You are
inclined to think it is neither that, nor any
other kind that you should trust yourself to,
but it is too late for consideration.

You roll out of Buffalo in the teeth of the wind,
and the world is turned to snow. All goes mer-
rily. The machine strikes little drifts, and they
scurry away in a cloud. The three engines
breathe easily, but by - and - by the earth seems
broken into great billows of dazzling white. The
sun comes out of a cloud, and touches it up
till it outsilvers Potosi. Houses lie in the trough
of the sea everywhere, and it requires little

imagination to think they are pitching and tossing before your eyes. The engines' respiration
is a little quickened. At last there is no more
road than there is in the Atlantic. A great
breaker rises right in the way. The monster,
with you in it, works its way up and feels of
it. It is packed like a ledge of marble. Three
whistles! The machine backs away and keeps
backing, as a gymnast runs astern to get sea-
room and momentum for a big jump; as a giant
swings aloft a heavy sledge that it may come
down with a heavy blow. One whistle! You
have come to a halt. Three pairs of whistles
one after another, and then, putting on all steam,
you make for the drift. The Superintendent
locks the door, you do not quite understand why,
and in a second the battle begins. The machine
rocks and creaks in all its joints. There comes
a tremendous shock. The cabin is as dark
as midnight. The clouds of flying snow put
out the day. The labored breathing of the locomotives behind you, the clouds of smoke and
steam that wrap you as in a mantle, the noon-
day eclipse of snow, the surging of the ship,
the rattling of chains, the creak of timbers
as if the craft were aground, and the sea getting out of its bed to whelm you altogether, the
doubt as to what will come next — all combine
to make a scene of strange excitement for a

land-lubber. You have made some impression upon the breaker, and again the machine backs for a fair start, and then altogether another plunge and shock and heavy twilight. And so, from deep cut to deep cut, as if the season had packed all his winter clothes upon the track, until the stalled trains are reached and passed, and then with alternate storm and calm and halt and shock, till the way is cleared to Erie.

It is Sunday afternoon, and Erie — "Mad Anthony Wayne's" old head-quarters — has donned its Sunday clothes, and turned out by hundreds to see the great plow come in — its first voyage over the line. The locomotives set up a crazy scream, and you draw slowly into the depot. The door opened at last, you clamber down, and gaze up at the uneasy house in which you have been living. It looks as if an avalanche had tumbled down upon it — white as an Alpine shoulder. Your first thought is, gratitude that you have made a landing alive. Your second, a resolution that if again you ride a hammer, it will not be when three engines have hold of the handle!

11

CHAPTER XI.

SNOW–BOUND.

THE law of association is a queer piece of legislation. There is the bit of road that used to extend from Toledo, where it connected with the steamer, stage and canal packet, to Adrian, Michigan, where stages took up the broken thread and jolted you on towards sunset. That road always suggests love-apples to the writer! Love-apples in those days, tomatoes in these. It was his first ride upon a railroad; and, reaching Adrian, he for the first time saw and tasted the beautiful fruit that, according to the newspapers, contains calomel and cancers. Was it a Persian pig, or some other, that offered a crown jewel for a new dish? Well, here was a new sensation, as strange as if the fruit that caused it had grown in Ceylon of "the spicy breezes." The hands that served them up are dust; the bit of road is lost in the great Lake Shore Line; the hamlet Adrian, with its log-cabin outposts, has grown a city with the flare and fashion of the latter day; but in the perishable tomato the memory of that first ride, that broad, burning August day, those pleasant friends, is assured forever.

There is the Road to Labrador, known as the Rome, Watertown & Ogdensburg, that deludes you in winter time from modern Rome, in the State of New York, and takes you into a world snowed clean of every fence and vestige of civilization, except houses in white turbans set waist-deep in the drifts. By-and-by the engine, with strange woodchuck proclivities, falls to burrowing in a white bank, and there you wait like a precious metal to be digged out. The wind gives Alaska howls around the shivering car. The stoves comfort themselves with a quiet smoke. The passengers scratch eyelet-holes in the frosted panes, and see hospitable farmhouses within shouting range, but as inaccessible as if they had been telescopic objects recently discovered in the moon. The lazy wood is frying with the comforting sound of a speedy meal. The brakemen stalk to and fro, and slam the doors, and are as talkative as sphinxes. The women bend around the departed fire like willows around a grave.

You wish you had Dr. Kane's "Arctic Explorations." A perusal of his coldest chapter might warm you a little. You get out into the snow, and flounder along to the engine. There it is, with its nose in the drift like a setter, and sings as feebly as a tea-kettle. The water drips through the joints of its harness, and hangs in icicles. Did you ever see an icicle grow? Now is your time. A drop of water runs down to the tip of the needle, halts and freezes. Then another, and another. Some get a little way, and give out. So the icicle grows bigger. Others manage to reach the point. So the icicle grows longer. It is about the only vegetable that grows downward, except Spanish moss. The engineer takes his dinner out of a little tin pail, and eats it before your eyes. The fireman keeps up the fire, and warms his feet before your toes. You ask the driver what is going to be done. He suspends the polishing of a chicken bone for a second, and says, "Waitin' for time!" Meanwhile the wind has been busy. It has chucked your hat into the bank, and filled it with snow, Scripture measure.

You go to the rear of the train and look back. You cannot see whence you came, nor how you ever *did* come, nor where you will ever get away. A brakeman starts out with a flag, and plods along the track. He need n't. There is nothing in the world that can come, and no more danger of colliding with a train than there is with the Fourth of July. He has started for

the last station, but he is in sight as long as you
can see him, and you could see him longer only
it is getting dark. By-and-by he returns, riding
on an engine that catches us by the heels and
drags us back to the station, where the hours
put a great deal of lead in their shoes, and stalk
slowly through the night. Two or three boys
come in. They are all of a bigness, like young
Esquimaux. They *are* Esquimaux. They stand
between you and the stove, and stare at you.
Like the moon, only one side of them is ever
visible, and that is the *fore* side. They are glad
there is a storm, glad the train is stopped. It's
fun. One of them has a basket of apples. You
buy some. You might as well try to eat a stal-
actite. They were frozen coming to the depot,
or before they started, or as soon as they ripened,
and you never knew when. Those boys laugh
at your discomfiture, and you hope there are
white bears in Labrador, and that one of them
is in a drift outside with a good appetite, and
that he will catch that apple-vender and empty
the basket and eat the boy! By-and-by the first
engine gives a frosty whistle and the second
engine gives another, and the conductor lets his
head in at the door and shouts "All aboard!"
as if he had been hindered all this while waiting for you to buy apples and wish for bears;
and the passengers clamber into the car and
huddle up, and away they go.

There is a lecturer on board, an itinerant vender of literary wares. He is as quiet as a statue, the coolest man in the party, and they are all half-frozen. At Pulaski, or Mexico, or some other foreign or ancient town upon that road, an audience awaits him. The Glee Club has sung itself out. The village boys have burned off their boot-toes on the red-hot stove. The blessed committee — if the town is large they number two, but if small, then five — have gone to the depot to catch the lecturer. He do n't come, so they try to strike him with lightning, but the wire is down and they miss him. The committee return to the hall and dismiss the hungry ears. The ears level objurgations at the lecturer — that word "objurgation" always reminds me of a club with a *knot* in it — and lift their skirts, and tie down their pantaloons, and trail themselves home. The train rolls in on muffled wheels at midnight, and the lecturer in it. But he does not land — not he — but keeps on to Oswego, where are more ears. During the day he hears from the committee. They want him to pay for lighting that hall, and making that fire, and printing those bills, and spoiling their course, and he pays it, and never more sees the halls of the Montezumas, if it be Mexico, or shrieks with Campbell's Freedom, "when Kosciusko fell," if it be Pulaski.

When thus snow-wrecked, there are several ways of getting warm without fire, though fire is best. And just here comes in that queer law of association. If reading about Dr. Kane's watch, that he handled with fur gloves because it was so cold it *burned* him, will not do, try Mungo Park toasting to death under an African tree, or fancy yourself wiping your brow with a dicky in the presence of an admiring audience, or sitting down upon your new hat in a lady's parlor —if none of these things will start the circulation, then nothing will do but fire. That experience of yours in Labrador occurred in early April, when bluebirds ought to be coming, and the sugar-bush bright with the camp-fire, and you think of a ride you took in another April long ago, upon the Memphis & Charleston Railway. You left Stevenson, a hamlet among the Cumberlands. The train was indigo-blue with soldiers. The country was wild with alarms. War may kill the husbandman, but it never halts the Spring. Life is bound to break in green surges along the woods and brighten the mountains. The air was warm as Northern June. The sky was soft as a maiden's eye — I don't mean Minerva — the sun unshorn of a tress of strength. You passed Huntsville, Alabama. You were in a country lovely as a pleasant dream. The flowers all abroad in the garden, a touch of gold upon the growing grain, the doors and windows all set wide open. The swift train, like a shuttle in a loom, wove the threads of green and blue, and the strands of sunshine, and the fancy-work of flowers, into one exquisite piece of tapestry, and laid it along the summer land. Out of the chill of the mountains, you washed your hands in the blessed air, all tinted and perfumed, and were glad. You left Nashville, Louisville, Indianapolis, Chicago, behind you. You are bound for La Crosse. Twenty-four hours ago it was June. Now it is March. The ground is frosted like a bridal loaf. The pastures are brown. The woods lift their giant arms in silent waiting.

The engine has run over parallels of latitude as if they were shadows, but it has done more. It has borne you from summer to winter in a round day. The stain of ripe strawberries is on your fingers, but your fingers are in mittens! We are all fashioned to live a great while in a *little* while, if we only know how. June and January are nearer together than any other brace of months in all the year. Show us the boy who, when he counts his temporal treasures and thinks of the Fourth of July, does not make a mental dive for his Christmas stocking the next minute!

CHAPTER XII.

SCALDED TO DEATH.

STEAM has ruined a great many things for us, and spoiled much poetry that was good and true in its time. The songs of the fireside to myriads are dead songs. What do they know about hearths and hickory, of backstick and forestick and topstick, and a great, cheerful fire, with a human smile and a human companionship in it, who camp around an unilluminated hole in the floor, and feel a gust of hot air like a simoon? Did you ever sit before a fireplace in a fall night — an eccentric philologist says that "autumn" is a better word than "fall"! — with somebody you owned to loving very much; sat an hour without speaking, and looked into the fire, you and he, you and she, and yet it seemed to you as if you had been talking all the while? It was the fire! No couple can sit and think thus around that defective spot in the floor, and enjoy it, unless they are idiots. Then steam has ruined the Iambic poetry of the flails, and sub-

12*

stituted therefor a gigantic smut-machine, that
runs wild in the field, and puts people's eyes
out, and gives them the consumption, and burns
up the wheat stack, and blows up the engineer.
Where is your champion cradler, that went in
with his skeleton fingers and laid out the grain
becomingly, after a Christian fashion? Dead.
Steam killed him. And what has become of the
reaper, and Longfellow's, and everybody else's
poetry about him? Cut to pieces with knives,
ground fine with wheels.

The clean and blessed fists that kneaded the
dough after a pugilistic fashion in the old days,
and moulded it into an eloquent answer to one
of the petitions in the Lord's Prayer, have forgotten their cunning — steamed to death. Enter
a Mechanical Bakery. Steam has bewitched
everything. Yonder are three, five, eight barrels
of flour tumbling about in a mass of dough that
would crush a district school, teacher and all.
No hands. There are doors opening in the two-
story oven, and cars laden with bread and crack-
ers come rolling out on a railroad track, and the
doors close behind them. No hands. Yonder
runs a train in at an open door. It will stay
in the hot chamber twenty minutes, and come
out of its own accord. The engine has burned
up the rolling-pin and the moulding-board, and
the big wooden cradle wherein they kept the

dough warm till it "rose" like any other member of the family; the fork wherewith the blessed biscuits and the mince-pies were tattooed like New Zealanders is thrown away, and the knife that marked the old oval shortcakes thus, ⋈, and without which household monogram shortcakes were *not* shortcakes, has followed the fork.

When they kindled a fire within the ribs of oak, and sent the steamer panting around the world, the old tradition of the ship was scalded to death. No more the tall masts cloud up, as the sky clouds, at the captain's word of command. No more does the breath of his trumpet roll up the piles of sails, volume above volume, and the nimble blue-jackets perched aloft swing themselves along the ratlines, and cling to nothing, like so many garden-spiders in their webs. It is a mimic storm of canvas, with Jack-tars instead of angels playing "in the plighted clouds!" Take a full-rigged ship, showing everything she can carry, and dressed in her best bunting, and watch her with a glass as she comes up into the horizon and stands squarely upon the visible sea, courtesying her way into the harbor like a high-born dame of the olden time! It is the stateliest thing, so far, of man's making.

Read of the naval battles that went long ago into song and story; of the great admirals; of Nelson and the rest; of the masterly manœu-

vering of McDonough and Perry and all the dead
Commodores that have made lake and sea mem-
orable, when they spread their great wings and
swooped down upon the enemy like sea-eagles.
It is grand to think of.   No machinery below
deck grinding away like a mill; nothing aboard
but the capstan, to heave in the cables and
bring the anchors home.   It must have been
something worth while to float a broad pennant
from a seventy-four, manned with a thousand
men! Steam and wheels have succeeded to the
old glories, and when you see a low-quartered
crocodile of a thing, black, unseemly, hugging
the water, and with a dingy-looking drum upon
its back, never despise it!   There is no telling
what it can do.   It is a turreted monitor in an
iron jacket, and carries a gun so preposterously
large, that it is not a boat with a gun in it, but
a gun with a boat to it.   It rips up your seventy-four as a rhinoceros an elephant, and sneaks
about under the guns unscathed.

Of guns: those Woolwich infants, as they call
them with a sort of grim facetiousness, that will
throw eight hundred pounds of iron seven miles!
As far as you can trot a horse comfortably in
an hour.   Could n't they be used to move an
iron-mine from one country to another?   These
devices, that steam and wheels are at the bottom of, brought into the service of Mars and

his tomahawk of a sister, Bellona, never seemed
to me so much the square and fair implements
of manly warfare, as infernal machines that ought
to be gathered up and packed away in the base-
ment of John Milton's "Paradise Lost," with
their makers just inside the door to keep watch
lest somebody should steal them! Then, again,
wheels are doing their best to trundle an exquisite Scriptural picture out of fashion. Ships
flock not so much "like doves to the windows,"
as tremendous forges afloat, with their pillared
smokes on high; the very cloud that came out
of the little bottle and took shape, and was the
greatest of the Genii in the Arabian Nights.

CHAPTER XIII.

ALL ABOARD !

A train on the Chicago & Northwestern Road
bound for California—a long, full train—a small
world on wheels. Everybody's double is aboard.
The first twenty-four hours settles things. The
little bursts of talk have given out. The great
monotone of the wheels sounds over all. In the
second twenty-four the small stock of gossip,
brought along fresh, is consumed with the last
crumbs of the home luncheon that was brought
along with it. People begin to show their grain.
One man is a bear. He falls back on the re-
serves, and sucks his paws for a living, and *win-
ters* through the trip. He isn't a playful bruin,
but he is harmless. He entered the car tolerably
plump. He leaves it intolerably lean. He is a
Spring bear.

Another falls to devouring books—he eats as
a horse eats, incessantly; he talks as a horse
talks, not at all—reads right through States, Ter-
ritories and deserts, over rivers, mountains and

plains. He might as well have gone to the Pacific in a tunnel.

See that woman in gray? A dormouse. She sleeps little naps fifty miles long, several times a day. She is an arrow of a woman — only aims at what she means to *hit*. A great many people are arrows: they get through the world with nothing to show for it.

Her neighbor is a knitter. Click, click, go the needles all day long. She would be glad to "knit up Care's raveled sleeve," or the hose for a fire-company. Wholesome to look at with her white cap and silver hair, but no more of a traveling companion than a cat.

Yonder is a motherly old lady, going to see a son in Iowa or Nebraska, and stay all winter. She lives in a house that has a lean-to and a great motherly kitchen, where they set the dough down on the hearth in its big wooden cradle, and make cider apple sauce by the barrel, and give you good, honest cheer. You can tell all this by her looks.

There's an old-time Eastern grandma. If any-body had told her twenty years ago she would ever wander beyond the Missouri River, she would have thought anybody an idiot. The loco-motive has done it, and is whisking her across the continent! She takes snuff. There is a faint suspicion of " Scotch" on her upper lip. She

takes out the shiny black box from her black
silk workbag — the shiny black box with a yellow picture of Queen Anne, or somebody in a
mighty ruff, upon the cover. She holds that box
in her left hand. She takes off the cover and
whips it under the box with her right. She
gives the side two little knocks with a knuckle.
The tawny titillative sets itself aright in the box.
There is something in the snuff looking like a
discomfited beetle, that shakes the yellow dust off
at her double knock. It is a vanilla bean. It
is a liberal box — liberal as her dear old heart —
and holds seventy-five sneezes! She offers it to
everybody within arm's-length. A true gentleman
who abominates snuff takes a dainty pinch with
a smile and a "thank you." So does a genuine
lady. But a saucy chit, of modern make, snuffs
contemptuously without taking any, and so does
a dashing sprig of a fellow who never had a
grandmother, and deserves none. This Old-World
courtesy over, grandma takes a pinch herself.
Watch her. She touches first this side, then that,
in a delicate way, with a thumb and finger,
shuts her eyes, and with two long comforting
snuffs disposes of the allowance. Mrs. James
Madison was a lady. So is grandma. Mrs. James
Madison took snuff and displayed two handkerchiefs, one for preliminaries, and the other, as
she herself said, "for polishing off." So does

grandma. One is cotton and blue, and the other is cambric and white. She sneezes. God bless her! Her life has been as harmless as a bed of sage, and as wholesome as summer-savory.

Is it a sin to take snuff? Not for grandma. There is no Bible prohibition for anybody, and not because Sir Walter Raleigh lived a while after Bible times, either. Neither were there railroads then, but here is an injunction to railway travelers, in case of accidents, as old as Hebrew: " *Their strength is in sitting still!* " The writer saw a man leave a car because it had broken loose from a train, jump head-first against a wood-pile, and knock his brains out. To make a cautious statement, he thinks those brains were a severe loss to the *owner*. The writer has seen a man weighing fourteen stone try to climb into the hat-rack to get out of harm's way, when the train left the track. Had the car turned over, there would have been *another* heavy cerebral calamity. ·

Yonder is a party of four around a little table. You catch fragments of talk about " decks " and " right-bowers," as if they were sailors ashore; " clubs," as if they were policemen; " kings " and " queens," like so many royalists; " going to Chicago," when they are all bound West; " tricks," as if they were conjurors. Then a laugh, somebody says " euchre!" and the game

13

and the secret are out together. An old man in a home-spun coat and a puzzled face watches the quartette. It is all Greek to him. He used to play "old sledge" when he was a boy, on the hay-mow of a rainy afternoon and nothing to do. The quaint face cards *look* familiar, but their conduct is inexplicable.

A man needs about as many resources on a long railway journey as Robinson Crusoe needed on that island of his. He wants a " man Friday" of some sort. If, like Mark Twain's Holy Land mud-turtles, he cannot sing himself, he must know how to make others sing. Have you never met a man who was a sort of *diachylon* plaster? Who drew you out in spite of yourself, and put you at your best, till you were not quite sure what he had been doing to you? That man knows how to travel. Two prime qualities go to the make-up of a successful tourist: the art of seeing and the art of listening. If, added to these, he understands the art of *telling*, then he is a triumph in a locomotive way.

But the wheels are beating the iron bars like a hundred hammers. It is a November night, and the icy rain drives sharply against the windows. The out-look is dreary enough. The Argumentative Man — there is almost always one on board — has gone to sleep. You know him.

He's the man who sits upon the seat in front of you, and overhears you make some statement to a friend — perhaps doctrinal. Your Argumentative Man is strong on doctrine. He wheels about on the seat, throws one leg over the arm, and picks you up. He addresses you as "Neighbor," or "Stranger,"— possibly "Colonel." If the last, you know whence he comes, and wish he would make himself the second, and are glad he is not the first. But he begins upon you. He quotes Paul at you, or Isaiah, or Genesis, or somebody. He crows over you. He gets upon his hind feet, and stands in the aisle and raises his voice, and looks around upon the half-dozen within ear-shot to challenge their admiration when he thinks he makes a point. He is the man that always lays his argument upon the thumb-nail of his left hand, leveled like an anvil, and then forges it every second or two with the thumb-nail of his right hand, and when he thinks he has you fast just holds one nail on the other a little while, as if it were *you* he had finished and was holding there till you got cool.

That man is exasperating. It is next to impossible to be a Christian where he is, and very hard to be a decent man. They give penny-royal tea to bring out the measles. He is a decoction of *human* penny-royal, and brings to the surface all the ill humors there are in you. Sometimes

your Argumentative Man is a clergyman, sometimes a layman, but you wish the train was a
ship bound for Tarshish, and the Man's name was
Jonah, and a convenient whale alongside, though
you are sorry for the whale — but then we are all
selfish, if we are *not* whales! But the Man
is asleep, and the knitting-work put away, and
the cards have had their last shuffle, and grandma is dreaming of home, and ever so many more
are gazing up at the car lights in a stupid way,
or looking out through the blank windows at —
nothing. The man with the black bottle is low-
spirited, so is the bottle, and he has settled his
head down between his shoulders — shut up like
a telescope. It is all dull and stupid enough.

There are two women seated together, plain
women, say forty-five or fifty years old. They
have good, open, friendly faces. Plainly dressed,
modest, and silent save when they conversed
with each other, you had hardly noticed them.
Perhaps there was the least touch of rural life
about them. They would make capital country
aunts to visit in mid-summer, or mid-winter for
that matter. If they were mothers at all, they
were good ones. So much you see, if you know
how.

Well, it was wearing on towards twelve o'clock
— the reader is requested to believe that this is
no fancy sketch — when through the dull silence

there rose a voice as clear and mellow and flexible as a girl's, of the quality that goes to the heart like the greeting of a true friend. It belonged to one of those women. She sat with her white face, a little seamed with time and trouble, turned neither to the right nor the left, seemingly unconscious that she had a listener. They were the old songs she sang — the most of them, — songs of the conference and the camp — such as the sweet young Methodists, and Baptists withal, with their hair combed back, used to sing in the years that are gone.

First it was

> "Rock of Ages! cleft for me,"

and then,

> "Our days are gliding swiftly on."

The clear tones grew rounder and sweeter. Those that were awake listened; those that were asleep awoke all around her. Some left their seats and came nearer, but she never noticed them. A brakeman, who had not heard a "psalm tune" since his mother led him to church by the hand when he was a little boy, and who was rattling the stove as if he were fighting a chained maniac, laid down the poker and stood still.

Then it was:

> "A charge to keep I have,"

and so hymn after hymn, until at last she struck up:

"I will sing you a song of that Beautiful Land,
  The far-away home of the soul,
Where no storms ever beat on the glittering strand,
  While the years of eternity roll.

"O, that home of the soul in my visions and dreams
  Its bright jasper walls I can see,
And I fancy but dimly the veil intervenes
  Between that fair city and me."

The car was a wakeful hush long before she had ended; it was as if a beautiful spirit were floating through the air. None that heard will ever forget. Philip Phillips can never bring that "home of the soul" any nearer to anybody. And never, I think, was quite so sweet a voice lifted in the storm of a November night on the rolling plains of Iowa. It is a year ago. The singer's name, home and destination no one learned, but the thought of one listener follows her with an affectionate interest. Is she living? Surely singing, wherever she is. I bid her Godspeed. She charmed and cheered the November gloom with carols of the Celestial City. She passed with the full dawn of the coming morning out of our lives, and there is a strange ache at the heart as we think so. Whoever heard her that night could write her epitaph. They could say —they could write:

SACRED

TO THE MEMORY

OF THE

WOMAN WITH THE SONGS

IN THE NIGHT,

CHAPTER XIV.

EARLY AND LATE.

SWIFT motion is the passion of the age. See a picture, see a statue, see a poem, the question is, How long did it take to do it? The press that does an old-fashioned month's work in thirty minutes; the method by which the engraver's patient labor, with skill in every touch of the burin, for a weary week, is counterfeited in fifteen minutes; the sewing-machine that kills one woman and does the work of twenty more, running up a seam like a squirrel up a limb; the railroad train that can stitch two distant places the most closely together — such are the things that kindle enthusiasm.

Did you ever see a man who had not ridden a mile a minute, or who did not think he had? ("A mile a minute" is a bit of flippant talk, like the man's who declared of a certain Fourth of July that he had seen a hundred better celebrations.) I never did, except two. One of them had never seen a locomotive, and the other con-

scientiously thought he went a *lit-tle* short of
fifty - nine.   A mile a minute has considerable
meaning.   It implies a velocity of eighty-eight
feet in a second.   It would keep a train ahead,
or at least abreast, of a brisk gale, so that there
would be no wind at all.   It would n't disturb
your front hair, my girl, if you stood on the rear
platform, and played Lot's wife by looking over
your shoulder.   It could n't catch you — at least
it could n't fan you — for it is a spanking gale
that makes sixty miles an hour in harness.

But everybody has gone a mile a minute by
the cars.   The writer has tried to tell a number
of people several times that *he* had ; that between New - Buffalo and Michigan City, on the
Michigan Central Road, and one of the noblest
and best - officered thoroughfares in the land, he
did go five miles in a minute apiece ; and he
went on explaining that the track was straight
as an arrow and smooth as glass, so that his
auditors might believe it and wonder over it, and
they all, one after another, rose and declared that
they had gone a mile a minute, and not one of
them as few miles as a paltry five !   Were you
ever standing on the deck of a sailing-craft, with
a brisk breeze blowing, when all at once it fell
to a dead calm, or went about so that your face
was swashed with the wet canvas, and your hat
knocked overboard ?   The writer was that unfor-

tunate navigator. So now he contents himself with telling that, years ago, he rode on a train of the old Toledo & Adrian Railway — strap-rail at that, where they had just half spikes enough, and pulled them out after the train passed, and drove them into the other end of the bars, to be ready for the engine when it returned — rode twelve miles an hour — a mile every five minutes; that it was good time, and everybody was proud of it. All of which was true. His auditors are all silent. He has the track; for if one of them ever rode any more slowly, he is ashamed to let anybody know it!

But there has not been the wonderful increase of speed on railways that we are led to think. Thus, thirteen years ago last May — 1860 — at the time of the Chicago Convention, the train bearing the Eastern delegates ran from Toledo to Chicago, over the Michigan Southern Road, two hundred and forty-three miles, in five hours and fifty minutes,—forty and a half miles an hour. It ran a match race with a train on the Michigan Central, and reached Chicago twenty-five minutes ahead. It was a great day for the late John D. Campbell, the Superintendent of the winning road, when, standing on the steps of the Sherman House in Chicago, he introduced the Superintendent and passengers of the belated Central to the crowd brought by the Southern, that were

14

there awaiting them. Poor Campbell! he has gone to the silent terminus of all earthly lines. Not long ago, Mr. Vanderbilt and party made a trip from St. Louis to Toledo, the engines doing their best. The distance is four hundred and thirty-two miles, the rate forty and one-tenth miles an hour, the actual running forty-five and a half — an average not decidedly favorable to continued health or remarkable length of days.

Locomotives never cultivate the grace of patience, though we should naturally think they would. The more engines there are to puff *for* us, the more *we* puff. We chafe at a detention of thirty minutes more than our grandfathers did, of thirty days. You know the man that always wants to go faster? Of the twin luxuries of high civilization, grumbling and the gallows, he enjoys grumbling best. His watch in one hand, his Guide in the other, and neither right, he compares the whereabouts of the one with the time of the other. He vows we are not going fifteen miles an hour when the rate is twenty-five if it is a rod. His chronic mania is to " *connect.*" He did n't " connect " yesterday, nor the day before, nor any other day, and he never will " connect " again as long as he lives. He is n't willing the engine should have a billet of wood or a drop of water. In fact, he is opposed to the train stopping at all, to let anybody off or on, until he has ridden out the last inch of his ticket. Denouncing collisions, he hopes that train Number One — *his* train is always Number One — will not wait a minute for Number Two, that is plunging on towards him upon a single track like a Devil's-darning-needle. " Have n't we got the right of way? " and that settles it.

The fellow has lost the *escapement* out of his mental watch-works, and he runs down as quick as you wind him up. Take him to pieces, and you will find he has none. Years ago, one of the staunch old Lake steamers made the quickest trip from Buffalo to Chicago then on the record of locomotion. Its passengers took a last look of New York and a first look of Chicago a little nearer together than anybody ever did before. The writer happened to be on the dock at Chicago when the steamer was nearing it. " Forward," was a man with a carpet-bag in his hand. He was a rusty man, as if he had been lost like a pocket-knife, and somebody had accidentally dug him up. He was trying to get over the guards somewhere, so as to jump ashore before the steamer " made a landing." He acted like an unruly steer trying to find a low place in the fence. Now, as it proved, he was the same man you always see in the cars, who wants to go faster. He had come from a Schoharie County

Hollow, where the sun never rises till eight o'clock and goes to bed two hours before night. He had driven a yoke of ruminants and hoof-dividers since childhood. He was going out West to see an uncle who did not know that he was coming, and would not have cared a straw if he *had* known. He had made the quickest voyage on record, but he was the original man who wants to go faster.

From the sacred to the profane is, as the world reads, like turning over a leaf in a book. Admiral Blake, a rough but noble old sea-dog, who used to take his steamer safely through as dirty weather as ever slopped a deck, saw this man, and, albeit not the president of any institution of learning, conferred the degree upon him then and there of D.D., the two letters being kept at a proper distance by a dash, and he gave him a name that could hardly have been his father's. It was the short word that Mr. Froude threw at the New York reporter's head when he asked the historian how he pronounced his name: " Like double o in fool, sir." The old Admiral's profanity is thus left scattered through this sentence in a fragmentary condition. It is hardly worth while to pick it up and adjust it.

Only this: I never could see the piety of

printing an oath with a *dash* in it. The wolf's
scalp is all you need to have to get the bounty.
To impale an oath upon a straight stick neither
hurts the oath nor helps the swearer. It is profanity by *brevet*, and ought to be banished from
the realm of type. If a man wants to write
" infernal," and he should not want to write it
unless it is proper, let him letter it squarely
out i-n-f-e-r-n-a-l, instead of sneaking into print
with the head and tail of it — in-f-n-l.

There used to be a picture that presented the
funny side of the man who is always a little late.
It showed a railway train rolling grandly out,
the fleeces of smoke dotting the route on the air
above it. Behind, at the distance of an eighth of
a mile, and losing ground every minute, as you
knew by his looks, was a man, his long hair
and his short coat-skirt leveled away behind him
like the two horizontals of the letter **F**. He
was after the train; he had been left, and those
railroad ties flew out from under his feet at a
lively rate. The engine enjoyed it, and the artist
helped to give expression to the creature's sat-
isfaction, for on every volume of smoke and
steam, in letters constantly growing smaller and
feebler as the clouds rolled farther and farther
away, like a faint cry in the distance, he had
written the words

" I 'VE GOT YOUR TRUNK ! "

" I 've got your trunk ! "

" I 've got your trunk ! "

" I 've got your trunk ! "

You could hear that jolly and saucy locomotive say every word of it.

The man who lets himself loose to pursue a train is a public benefactor. Everybody is pleased with the performance — but the performer. The

A LITTLE LATE!

loungers on the platform at the station encourage him with shouts that put " spurs in the sides of his intent." The engineer leans out at his window and lets the engine whistle for him, and sometimes slackens a little, just by way of delusive encouragement. The brakeman on the rear platform seems to be putting on the brakes with

might and main, to hold · the train for him to
catch it. Passengers beckon to him, and wave
him on with hand and handkerchief. When he
lags a little, the observers cheer him, and he
dashes on in prodigious bursts of speed. Boys
whirl up their hats and bet he 'll win. But
his heart begins to kick like an unruly colt, and
he comes to a halt and stands like a mile-post
and stares after the receding train. Then he
turns and, mopping his face with his handkerchief,
walks slowly over the course. He does not seem
anxious to reach the depot, although by the
laughing of the crowd he knows they are all
glad to see him coming. He can count more
teeth than he ever saw at one time, except in a
Saginaw gang-saw mill. But he seems to shrink
in a modest way from the greeting he is so
sure of.

Now there were Christians in that crowd.
There must have been. There were in Sodom.
There are everywhere except among the Modocs.
But I am afraid there was not a Christian on
that train or about that station that in his secret heart wanted that man to catch the cars
—that could have prayed for the achievement,
no matter what depended upon it, and kept his
countenance.

CHAPTER XV.

DEAD HEADS.

" D. H." Everybody knows what D. H. is. He sees it on the telegram that costs him nothing. He sees it in the glass when he looks at himself, if he rides free upon the train — Dead Head. It never had a pleasant sound, and lately it has grown almost opprobrious. In the beginning, the courtesy of a pass was extended to the drivers of the quill. The editor and his family and his wife's mother and the pressman and the devil all rode scot-free.

Then State Lycurguses *en masse* with their families and their mothers-in-law, members of every house of Congress, all kinds of Judges, all people that were " their Excellencies," or " Honorables," *very* rich men that could buy a couple of hundred miles of the road and not mind it, and last, clergymen. These were classed with children under eight years old, for they went at half-fare — rode one half mile for nothing and paid for the other half. The ground of this fractional manifestation of grace is debatable. Possibly it was poverty, and if poverty, then to the shame of the churches that ·received the earnest and incessant labors of men, and then sent them out begging for a living. It is a hard, ugly word, but it is the true one.

At length when, upon a single line of road, six thousand people were all riding at once fare-free as a flock of pigeons; and when people who held "complimentaries" were asked to hold their tongues when they ought to tell the truth, and shut their eyes when they ought to keep them open; and when editors began to discover that their passes made them about the cheapest commodities in the market, and that, by reason of the bit of pasteboard, they were doing more work for less money than anybody else in America, then there began to be a lull in the pass-system. Railroad Companies had spasms of resolutions that they would confer the degree of D. H. upon nobody. That was incredible, for when a railroad finds it for its *interest* to issue a pass, you may believe the pass will be forthcoming without a pang. But the clergymen's half-loaf always seemed to me a sort of half-handed charity that should have been resented, in a Christian way, instead of being accepted. That, to-day, they generally recognize the fact that the people who do not pay them should furnish their tickets,

15*

instead of the people who never heard of them till they produced their credentials in order to be numbered with the infants, is a more truthful and manful view of the situation.

There are D. H.'s beyond the meaning of the railways. There was a church in Otsego County, N. Y., with as many brains and as much grace in it as in any country church of its time. It had a minister, faithful, able, earnest, who preached out-and-out and through-and-through Bible sermons. He was not a "star-preacher." He knew little about astronomy save the Star of Bethlehem. That man preached forty years for that church, and they never paid him a dollar. They made "bees," and drew up his winter's wood, and cut his grain. That was all.

Well, he was gathered to his fathers, but he had spoiled the church. He had educated it to be D. H. without knowing it. After he died, the deacons went looking about for a two-hundred-and-fifty-dollar minister, and you can get about as much minister for that price as you can get psalm-tune out of a file. Finally they tried five hundred dollars' worth. It was a cheap article they got. It was hard to hear him preach, but harder for them to pay him for it. They had been deplorably educated. They were Dead-Heads.

Their church edifice stands to-day on a hill,

like the Celestial City, but it is a very dilapi-
dated one. If you go there any summer Sunday, you shall find it untenanted save by the
fowls of the air. They had a funeral there last
season, for Death opens the old building sometimes, and on a window-ledge near where the
gray-haired singers used to strike up "Mear"
and "Corinth" and old "China," a mother-bird
—a robin—sat undisturbed upon her nest. The
good old Elder's grave across the road is sunken
and weed-grown. "So runs the world away."

Writing of churches: By a sort of common
consent, Modocs seem to be excepted from any
general plan of salvation but the *Quaker* plan.
The writer once went as far West as the railroad could carry him, and then took the bare
ground into Nebraska till he struck the Indian
country, and found a Mission twenty years old
in the wilderness. It is probable that very few
of them deserved baptizing, but they all wanted
washing. Having heard the little Indians sing
hymns, you went about a mile and saw where
they had buried a horse, that the dead brave
might make a good appearance on the Happy
Hunting Grounds, which they thought he would
reach in about fourteen days.

You saw red-ochre fellows who were well up
in the three R's—"reading, 'riting and 'rithme-
tic"—who had slipped back into the old burrows

as naturally as woodchucks. You saw one young man, tolerably educated, who had served in the Federal army, and served well, sunning himself on the turfed slope of a summer wigwam. All that was left of his civilization was the tatters of a pair of blue pantaloons. He had slipped back into his blanket, and felt as much at home in it as a fawn in his spots, though the comparison is greatly damaging to the fawn. You ask him about this advance backwards, and he says, " 'Mong white folks nothin' but *Ingen.* 'Mong Ingen *nobody*—come back tribe be good Ingen as any." And you have the situation clearly stated for your consideration.

You ask the missionary how many of the tribe he counts as Christian. He enumerates, and you wish to see one. He points him out, a villainous-looking old fellow with a lowering eye, and the most of his head packed like a knapsack behind his ears, and you think a little preliminary hewing and scoring would hardly come amiss to make him a safe man to meet in the night-time, and trim him down to Christian proportions. Say, with a hatchet, hew to a line commencing just in front of his organ of self-esteem, and make a clean sweep of things to a point just back of his ears. There would then be a better organization to begin upon. After that, Robert Raike's recipe, plenty of water with soap

in it, would be in order. Then try catechisms.
Catch an Indian young, and something may be
made of him if he does n't get away, but an old
Indian is a tough creature to tame. You felt
like asking the missionary if, this man being a
Christian, there were many *sinners* near by. If
so, it seemed prudent to get back to the railroad without standing very particularly upon "the
order of your going."

CHAPTER XVI.

WORKING "BY THE DAY."

SOMETHING is written elsewhere of the grave-yard luncheons they took in the Sunday noonings. Those were the times when the minister worked by the day. The Sunday school in the morning, for the lambs led off the flock. Then a hymn on both sides of the threshold of prayer, and a little carpet of Scripture laid down before it. The preacher would read the hymn, and say, " Sing five verses;" and if he did not happen to put up the bars in this way across the narrow lane of praise, the choir were bound to sing it through, if it was as long as " The Ancient Mariner." Then the sermon, wherein there was a world of scoring and hewing, and showers of chips that hit people here and there, and the work was laid out generally. Then another hymn, the prayer and the benediction. This took till high noon. Then afternoon, wherein the morning's frame was put together, mortise and tenon each adjusted in its own place, raised, roofed and sided, and a doctrine or so put into it to keep house.

The afternoon was the forenoon over again, except that the grandest of all mere human breaths of praise, the Doxology, was sung, and "the disciples went out." The congregation always stood when the clergyman called upon the name of the Lord; and sometimes he called a long time, and occasionally a feeble body, and now and then a lazy one, went down like a forest before a mighty wind! Is there any becoming posture in public prayer between kneeling and standing? Is it not either the one extreme or the other? To see a congregation with their heads every way, like a field of barley after a hail-storm, does not inspire a sentiment of reverence; but a people rising to their feet as one man is an impressive act of homage. Then the Bible class was chinked in somewhere between songs and sermons, and the conference-meeting came in the evening, and held till nine o'clock. For a day of rest, the old-fashioned Sunday was about as busy as a meadow full of hands with the hay down and a storm coming!

Once in four weeks was covenant-meeting. It occurred on Saturday afternoons, began at one, and lasted till four or five. The little boys of good people in the writer's childhood had to go to covenant-meeting. The writer's parents were

good people, and *he* went. The reader is requested to remember that Saturday afternoon
was the old-time holiday—the only day in the
week when the small animal, man, could kick up
its heels with the halter off. There is no recollection more vivid and more painful than of
those tremendous Saturday afternoons. I had
heard of Joshua, and I couldn't persuade myself
that he was dead, though I wickedly hoped he
was, for somebody must have commanded the
sun " to stand still," and it obeyed.

The laugh of the children of the perverse generation came faintly and sweetly from the neighboring orchard. The rays of the sun streamed
aslant through the still air of the church like
the visible ladder of glory, but not to the rest-
less eyes that watched, but only the token of the
expended day, and no other to be had till the
last of next week. It was the later covenant
the church members were renewing, but the old
covenant made by the Lord with Noah would
have been far preferable. There was something
beautiful to look at about that—the seal of the
covenant—the Bow of Seven. As it seems, now,
there was a blunder somewhere.

There was nothing upon wheels in that church.
The shepherd stayed by his flock till his hair
silvered, and his deacons were as gray as he.
No clergyman was on wheels but the Methodist.

Had the gauge been right, and had there been railroads, it would have been convenient to have casters attached to the boots of the clergymen of that faith and order, for so they could be trundled away at will like pieces of heavy furniture!

There was a time when people put on their slippers, took a night-lamp, bade each other good night, and went up stairs to bed. Those people now go to bed by railway. They think nothing of fifty miles between counting-room and bedroom. They die out of the city every evening, and are born into it with newness of life every morning. It is a good thing. They live more, and they live longer, if the engine behaves itself; but when it gets a notion to pass a sister engine on a single track, or to try the bare ground, like a horse with his shoes off, that kicks up its heels in the pasture, or to climb aboard the train and be a passenger itself, perhaps the bedroom may be a few miles too far away, and the old geography be best.

There was a time when we kept our dead about us; in sight of the church windows where folks went in the Sunday noons to eat their luncheon, and leaned against gray slabs and read the dim-lettered records of the hamlet's forefathers, and talked about the sermon and the — crops. They had observed that things kept growing on

Sundays, and they mentioned it! If not in sight
of the church windows, then just in the edge of
the village, a pleasant stroll after tea, where old
people walked and looked grave, and young people sat and talked low, not so much about the
mute Miltons or the village Hampdens, as an article, or so they fancied, situated somewhere under
the left half of their jackets and bodices. Now,
from "sanitary" considerations — I think that is
the word — they have located the cemetery so far
away that you must buy a ticket to reach it.
When first they began to hurry the dead to the
grave at the rate of thirty miles an hour, it *did*
give the old-time sense of the proprieties a little
wrench, but it was not an outright fracture of
anything, and so the proprieties were long ago
convalescent.

CHAPTER XVII.

A SLANDERER AND A WEATHER MAKER.

THE Railroad is a slanderer. It maligns cities. With few exceptions it *sneaks* into town; enters it by the cheapest end, as politicians say of candidates, the most "available" way. By-the-by, is the "available" aspirant for office always the cheapest? It comes in by people's backdoors; it sees mops swinging like "banners on the outer wall;" it overlooks hen-houses; it flanks pig-pens; it manufactures dead ducks and gone geese; it commands barnyards. Take La Porte, on the Lake Shore Railroad — one of the most beautiful little cities in the whole West, *nothing* excepted. Its streets are pictures. Its shade is luxuriant. Its lakes are lovely as any classic water that ever inspired a poet's song. Ask the world that flits by on the Lake Shore, and never halts at all, about La Porte, and it says, a straggling Hoosier village, out at the elbows and the heels withal, fringed with shanties, mopsticks and swill-pails. And on he plunges in his ignorance, knowing as little of the Gem of the Prairie as if he had been born, like a Mammoth Cave fish, without any eyes at all. The Michigan Central and the Illinois Central Roads, in their approach to Chicago, are splendid exceptions. Running on the water side and out at sea, if you please, they pass along the city front, with its stately structures, its spires and towers, as if it were a magnificent painting. By night, when garlanded with lights, it is as gorgeous as some Eastern queen arrayed in all her jewels.

There are in America at least six hundred and forty railroads, without counting the branches. Of the latter there are hundreds, and it is curious to observe how certain trunk roads resemble trees in putting out their branches and getting their growth. Thus the iron arms of the Michigan Central spread like a larch, the Chicago & Northwestern like a fern, while the Hudson River takes a straight shoot as limbless as a liberty-pole. We are apt to crowd the rhetoric sometimes, and say that railroads have taken America, and the continent is as full of fibres of iron as an oak leaf is of fibres of wood. I saw a letter the other day written by a Bishop of the Episcopal Church from his home here in America. That letter traveled a thousand miles before it struck a railroad! His diocese is in the Hudson's Bay Company's country, and is no looryard diocese either, for it is larger than many empires.

But the locomotive ventures into improbable places for all that. Think of a ponderous engine, fashioned to grind miles under its wheels like a grist in a mill, being drawn, as one was a short time ago, under the Arch of Constantine at Rome, along the very road whereon the robe of Cicero trailed, if he didn't lift it, and the weak-eyed poet strolled! Classic ground or Holy ground, it stands a poor chance with the locomotive, for with the steam comes the newsboy, the boot-black, modern slang, irreverence, and — peanuts.

No piece of mechanism has affected so widely, diversely and powerfully, the globe and its inhabitants, as the locomotive. That a railroad should influence the weather is the very last thing that would be suspected, but it must plead guilty to the charge, for in certain regions it is almost *climatarchic* — a presider over climate. That being the only *hard* word used, the offence should be easily forgiven. Let some recording angel, like Uncle Toby's, be found to drop a tear upon it, if need be, and blot it out.

Everybody knows how the rains have descended and the floods come in regions of the continent and in seasons where and when little ever fell but dew. Number the facts from Utah to California that are being washed down into human understandings by heavy showers. There is no danger of our being claimed by Sydney Smith's genuine Mrs. Partington, if we say that some-how—and we are not bound to tell how—the railroad brings rain. Would it not be wonderful if that brace of iron bars across the continent should literally interpret the pleasant Scripture, "And the desert shall blossom as the rose"? And it looks like it. The old devices for arti-ficial irrigation are growing useless, and territory hitherto unproductive, is beginning to do some-thing for man. And this, not because of the pioneers to whom the railroad has made the desert possible and accessible, but because of its direct influence upon the climate. Rain-clouds west of the Rockies, that have never spoken a loud word within the memory of man, are now talking as audibly and emphatically as if thunder had been their mother-tongue from babyhood, and rank vegetation is springing where nothing was ever before sown but fire.

The vast system of iron net-work and the hair-lines of telegraphy, about enough to make a snare to catch the planet, have disturbed the electrical equilibrium, and the results are seen in the new and novel phenomena of thunder and shower. By the way, did you ever know any part of a train to be struck by lightning? There are three or four accounts on record of such an occurrence, but the testimony is doubtful and obscure. Running in what are generally deemed the most dangerous places, along the tall fences of telegraph-poles, so often shattered by lightning, and throwing up such volumes of heat, smoke and steam, all of which are supposed to be favorite thoroughfares of the mysterious agent, it seems strange that, if our scientific facts *are* facts at all, many accidents by lightning do not occur upon the railway. But the direction of the bolt is determined before it leaves the cloud, and a train is nothing but a slender thread trailed along the earth's surface. What the locomotive will yet do for all kinds of man—mechanic, agricultural, scientific, moral—is an unsolved problem! A glance at the initial chapter of its history assures us that it will be as marvelous in the future as it was unlooked for in the past.

CHAPTER XVIII.

DREAMING ON THE CARS.

WHEN a man travels, what material baggage he takes is *im*material, but he leaves behind him a great deal of mental and moral *impedimenta.* There used to be a saying among the traders to Santa Fé, "If there is any dog in a man he will show it out on the trail." During the war, people going to the front were astonished to learn what manner of people some of their nearest neighbors really were. It is so in the world on wheels. Men and women show out wonderfully. But whatever you put on to go a-journeying, even to that new silk hat, if you must, never put on *airs.* They are altogether too gauzy to be warm in winter, or decent in summer. Many a woman has told you, without intending it, that the entertainment she regarded with such measureless contempt is better than anything she ever encountered at home. Clothes have become transparent as window-glass. They utterly fail as a disguise.

You grow conscious on a railway train, as nowhere else, what trifles go to make up the warp
and woof of life. Thus, you catch yourself
watching an old-fashioned man with an ancient
hat that was beaver in its time. He takes it
off and holds it in his hand. You wonder how
it has come to look so like its owner. It has a
character, and the character is the man's. Then
the heavy roll of his coat-collar, with a padded
look, reminds you of the picture of George the
First, the Last, and the All-the-Time, to-wit:
George Washington. You think G. W.'s face is
much like a tin lantern with no holes in it to let
out the light, and about as — is it profanity, or
what is it? — about as *stupid* a face as there is
going. To be sure, it has a solid look, and so
has a round of beef.

You look up just then, and, yonder in the
corner facing you, sits a man of sixty, frosty,
Octoberish, square face, double chin, hair long
and curly, pleasant eyes, all surmounted by a
broad-brimmed hat. You start at the resem-
blance; it is as much like Benjamin Franklin,
printer, as one picture is like another.

Then you wonder what that lady over across
the aisle is trying to get out of that bottle with
a knitting - needle. You watch, and she spears
away until she brings out a little pickle. You
notice a couple whispering and giggling, and

17

making objects of themselves generally, and you marvel why, when young married people travel in the cars by sunlight, they don't let the honeymoon set, or change, or something.

The train stops at a station among the pines — you are on a Wisconsin road — and little girls come to your window with small clusters of wintergreen berries, set off with a few glossy leaves. You buy a fresh woodsy taste of spring, and then follow the girls away to their humble homes among the sand-hills, and fancy how they live and what they hope.

The train halts at a station in Maryland — you are on the train from Washington to New York — and dusky boys and maidens, born on the shady side of humanity, swarm around with neat little paper-boxes, with a layer of fried oysters looking as light and frisky as your grandmother's fritters. The ivory smiles are very pleasant to see, and before you know it you are humming " Way down in Alabama," and sorrowing that some of the sweetest melodies in the world since the daughters of Judah hung their harps on the willows, should have dropped out of fashion like lead down a shot - tower, and wondering what poet, what historian, will yet preserve the legends and songs of the days of the Old Plantation. Then you wander away to Holy Land, and consider what punishment should be meted out to

the man who has just been telling us — and
wants to be thanked for it!—that the trees those
Jewish Girls hung their harps on — those sweet-
voiced girls, with the blue-black hair — were not
willows at all, but *poplars!* Old-fashioned people call them "popples." Fancy a singer hanging her harp on a popple! Then, there is now
and then a lady who has a sort of petroleum-
fortune refinement, who speaks of a poplar-tree
as a "popular," much as if she should fancy
that engineer is a sort of corruption of *indianeer.*
All these things are dreadful, but a popple-hung
harp is worse.

The train pulls up at a station in Virginia,
and a barefoot girl approaches you with flowers
to sell — fragrant Magnolias, and the most graceful and grateful offering of all, and you fall to
thinking if anything so beautiful will ever be
named after you, as this magnolia was, after that
Professor Magnol. Happy Magnol! The flowers
should grace his tablet in the fairest of white
marble. Now you pass through the apple region
of New York, and the chestnut woods of Ohio.
You know both, by the swarms of small Buck-
eyes bearing chestnuts, and the bits of Excelsiors
loaded with Greenings and Baldwins.

Then you fall to watching the man with the
new silk hat. Every body does. It is not an
irritated hat, for it shines like a bottle. He

bought it yesterday, and is going a thousand miles immediately. The head seems to have been made just to have some handy place to put the hat. That hat thus put comes into the car. Its support is seated, carefully applies a thumb and finger to both sides of the brim, and lifts it perpendicularly off, much as if his ears ran up into the top of it, and he would lift it away without touching their tips. He looks at it. It caught a little bump as he entered the car, and there is the mark. He smooths it with a finger in a sorrowful way, reaches up, and puts it in the rack *crown* down. Then he settles to the journey, thinks again, elongates, and puts that hat *brim* down. This satisfies him.

In a few minutes he rises, gives that castor another turn, as if it were a kaleidoscope and he bound to have one peep more, and deposits it upon its side. At the instant he is about to let go of it the car gives a frolicsome lurch, and that hat catches a jam. He withdraws it tenderly, and there is the scar. It *looks* like the kick of a vicious horse, but it *is* the work of an ass to wear such a thing on a journey. What sort of a figure would Moses have cut with a silk hat, in the last years—say the thirty-eighth of them—of his Wilderness wanderings? Well, the man whips out his handkerchief, and allays the irritation of the angry hat. He applies his tongue to it as if for some healing quality, claps it upon his head, and, wearied with physical exertion and mental anxiety, falls asleep. He is *not* Jupiter, but he resembles him, for he " nods," and that unhappy tile tumbles, strikes the back of the seat with the *thrum* of a feeble tambourine, and bounds sepulchrally along the floor. A man puts his foot upon it in his haste to be neighborly, and " when the man with it" recovers the unlucky bit of head-gear, it looks like a short-joint of stove pipe that somebody has wildly hammered and wickedly sworn at because it would neither go inside nor outside. But the man with the new silk hat never falters. He carries a head to put the hat on. He carries a hat-box to put the hat in. He makes a right angle of himself, and sets his hat right side down upon his lap, as if about to play an endless game of " pin." You saw him yesterday. There is " an eternal fitness in things," even in *hats.*

They used to tell — in old times more than now — of " presenting the freedom " of this and that, London or Amsterdam, or what not, to somebody " in a gold box." That is not the ceremony in later days. They present you " the freedom " of the world on wheels, if you can pay for the *ticket.* On a California-bound train you met a lady. Not to indulge in any pleasant euphemism, she was a half century old, but then she was strong and womanly, and apparently no nearer death than when she was handed about in long-clothes. She was the mother of men. She was the wife of an English physician and botanist; I should say "scientist," but if there is a mean word in the language, it is that same "scientist." It reminds me of nothing but a thin, offensive bug, that has been subjected to the pressure of a vindictive thumb-nail. She was unattended. She had a ticket that shut over and over like a Japanese book. It was good from London to — New Zealand! Across two oceans, Atlantic and Pacific; across the American continent. She was bound home. She ate strawberries, she said, with her husband and "the boys," just before she left New Zealand. She ate strawberries with her sister at the parting meal in London; and, as she smilingly added, "I shall be in time for strawberries and cream at San Francisco."

No more nervous anxiety about the lady borne on wheels around the globe, than if she had been walking under the palms in her Australasian home. You could not help thinking, as you regarded her pleasant face, of the Malay of the old Geography dressed in a towel, amidst a far-away and inaccessible scene of tropic luxuriance, only to be found after months of tossing by sea and perils by land, of cannibals and beasts of prey; and here she was, going directly there to her charming English home in the South Pacific seas, with that crown-jewel of the firmament, the Southern Cross, in sight. How pitifully shriveled, like a last year's filbert, is Tom Moore's little song about the Irish Norah, who went on foot and alone around the Emerald Isle unharmed —

> "On she went, and her maiden smile
> In safety lighted her round the Green Isle"—

beside the tremendous arc of circumnavigation the Doctor's wife was describing without a flutter!

So all these trifles beguile the way, keep the mental watch from running down in your pocket, until the brakeman earns his supper by telling you where you can earn yours, as he shouts through the car, "Twenty minutes for supper!"

CHAPTER XIX.

"MEET ME BY MOONLIGHT."

THERE were two steamers on Lake Erie that
were twins. They were, in their time, and not so
long ago, models of steamboat architecture; elegant as palaces, and in every respect as nearly
alike as builders and artists could make them.
Their names were *Northern Indiana* and *Southern
Michigan.* The writer and "his next best friend"
took passage upon one of them bound East. It
was a mid-summer night. The moon at the full,
and her ladyship did what all poets, since moons
and poets were, have said she did — made day,
"only a little paler" and lovelier, and what not.
The steamer was running her sister's trip, that
sister having met with an accident. The damage
being repaired, it was proposed that, when the
twins met on this voyage, the passengers should
be transferred from each to the other, the sisters
wheel about. and retrace the wake they had just
made, and so the advertised trips for the season would come all true again.

The sea was as nearly a sea of glass as it ever is. The moon rode high in the heavens. It was just midnight when we saw the sister coming, decked with white and colored lights alow and aloft, like a queen of "the barbaric East" in all her jewelry. The lights from two stories of windows streamed out upon the air. The music of the band was heard. It looked like a city adrift, and beautiful and airy as a dream. Our deck was thronged with passengers, who saw themselves in the approaching apparition as *others* saw them. They were looking upon the steamer's counterpart and double.

The two neared each other, came alongside in the middle of the sea, the planks were put out fore and aft, and the transfer of passengers and baggage began. There were two steady currents of human life meeting and passing on the gangway. Age, youth, beauty, fashion, wealth, poverty. Bright lamps shone all around, and the moon over all. People looked in each other's eyes, glanced at each other's faces, as they met for an instant, sometimes gravely, sometimes with a smile, that nevermore in all this world would meet again. Now and then a pleasant word was uttered between strangers, but generally the two processions were silent, almost thoughtful. It was a scene at once beautiful and impressive. The occupants of State Room B in

18*

the *Northern Indiana* found themselves occupants of B again in the *Southern Michigan*. The passengers in the upper cabin of the one found all unchanged in the upper cabin of the other. " The places that once knew them should know them no more forever." The transfer was effected with less confusion than in a congregation leaving a church. The bells rang a parting chime. The steamers wheeled, each upon her own route. We had died out of one world into another. It was a picture of life and of death on the moonlit sea. Such as it was, can I ever forget it?

The memory of the first steamer you ever saw comes dimly out, like a smoky old picture. Let us say it was the steamer *Nile*, with a bronze-faced old sea-dog for captain; the steamer *Nile*, with two gold crocodiles on the bow for a figure-head; the steamer *Nile* at her dock in Buffalo, and " up" for the City of the Straits. The rush of crowds and steam, the farm-wagons laden with household gods and goods that were backed over the broad gangway; the shy country horses that were pulled and pushed aboard; the Mrs. John Rogerses, " carrying one for every ten" by the old rule of addition; the score of sheep, frightened out of their little wits, huddled together forward; the sailors coiling lines and chains; the close, dim cabins lined with berths; "the walking-beam" working slowly up and down; the faint, hot smell of steam and oil; the wheezy way with the machinery; the little leaks of steam and water here and there that snuffed and hissed, above and below, as if everything about the craft were alive and generally uneasy.

Then came the clang of the bell and the voice of the first mate, "All ashore that's going!" The captain in position on the hurricane deck; a tinkle of bells in the engine-room; the rasp of the lines the sailors pull in with a will; a general jail delivery of steam; leviathan moves; she is off; the flags unroll to the wind; the band on deck strikes up "Charley over the Water;" the great crowd of men and women and horses and drays upon the deck gets the size of a swarm of bees on an apple-tree limb; then a mere handful of hornets; then out of sight. Every time the wheels come about, the boat shakes as Cæsar shook with that Spanish fever of his, when he called Titinius; up stairs and down stairs an incessant rumbling and tumbling that make things jingle. You are fairly at sea; the air is fresh and clear, as if just made. The *Nile* was a grand affair in her day, but as Egyptian as the New York Tombs. She laid her bones on the Michigan beach one terrible night; and her old commander, ill ashore, lived just long enough to hear of it.

Who were aboard? Elder Alfred Bennett, for one—not Reverend, nor yet New Jersey Bishop —but *Elder* Bennett, with a head like Humboldt's, and holding more of celestial geography than the great Baron knew of earthly—a lion of the tribe of Judah. Of all titles for Baptist clergymen, "minister" seems to me the simplest and most suggestive. It associates them with "the ministering spirits" of whom we read, and whom we believe in. Take a young fellow from Hamilton or Rochester, who never tarried six weeks at Jericho, and call him Elder, as his country brethren and sisters always will, and there is an amusing incongruity about it, as if the old proverb, "the child is father of the man," had come literally true, and the downy Elder's father were a little boy somewhere, about big enough to figure in the Millennial group of the leopard and the lamb.

Father Bennett was bound for Michigan. He would see that accomplished Christian gentleman, Dr. Comstock. He would see that noble preacher and large-hearted man, Rev. John I. Fulton; he would see Elder Powell, one of the Thirteen who gave a dollar apiece, and so founded Madison University. He would return to Utica, and meet that admirable Editor, Dr. A. M. Beebee, of the New York *"Baptist Register;"* in youth, office-mate with Washington Irving, the man of Sunnyside; in manhood, the thorough, consistent, able Christian editor. He would consult with Dr. Nathaniel Kendrick, that giant in the churches; with Professor Hascall, who took Madison University into an upper chamber, as the disciples gathered, and kept it till its name was strong enough to go abroad, and was worked for and prayed for all at once, as the "Ham. Lit. and Theo. Sem." Elders Card and Cook would come down to meet him from the North Woods; Elders Galusha and Moore and Hartshorn from the West. They would all attend some Association together, and Elder John Peck, as clean-hearted as an angel, always had a word to say. He was one of the great noble provocatives to good works, and had he never achieved anything himself but that, the "well done, good and faithful servant!" would have been the verdict. But Elder Peck never *could* say "Association." You can shut your eyes and hear him: "the brethren of the *As-so-sa-shun* will please to give their attention." All these — Elder Powell, perhaps, excepted — have gone away to the Great Convention of the church triumphant.

Are people's memories getting shorter? Does anybody remember how Dr. Kendrick used to begin one of his old heart-of-oak sermons? How he towered up behind the low pulpit, like a Lombardy poplar behind a fence? How that two-story head of his reminded you of the portrait of Oberlin! The first words came slowly and ponderously. Those silver-rimmed spectacles shone around his eyes. He laid out his work by the day, and not by the job. He told you of "the damning demerit of sin." He climbed rugged Sinai like a stout mountaineer. By-and-by away went the spectacles. He warmed and softened to the work. His words came fast. He descended Sinai and went away to Gethsemane. And when he was through, and occasionally it took him a long time, you felt that you had heard a man of remarkable power, who had yet a store of it in reserve — a man who could handle the doctrinal sledge with one hand, and never strain a muscle.

Dr. Kendrick, like many of that class of old divines -- as witness Dr. Backus, of Hamilton College -- had a world of ready wit, that flashed out unexpectedly from the soberest of mouths. One day of the dead days, the Doctor was conducting a class in Moral Philosophy, and he asked a student if a man could tell a lie to a brute. The student *thought* not, and so put his foot in it and *said* "not." "Once," said the Doctor, in his deliberate way, "I visited a ministering brother in the western part of this State. In the morning he took a halter, and went into the pasture to catch his horse. He hollowed an empty hand and extended it. The horse pricked up his ears at the prospect, came up, thrust his nose into the barren hand and was captured. Some time after, I was called to sit in council in that same region. The minister alluded to stood charged with having made misrepresentations to his fellow-men. I am sorry to say the allegations were proved true. *I* had seen him practice deception upon a quadruped. *They* had heard him tell a falsehood to a biped. Now," added the Doctor, " were the two acts alike, or did the hind legs of the quadruped kick out the brains of the intent?" The class laughed, but the student did n't say!

CHAPTER XX.

THE MAKER OF CITIES.

No matter how carefully you freight a train, there is always something gets on board that never appears on the bill of lading. Day after day you see Alexandrine caravans pounding away to Iowa, burdened with Michigan forests that sawmills have laughed over in their rough, coarse way. It is called lumber, but it *is* a county capital, a whole village, a happy home. Score out with the double bars of the railroad a broad page of the open book of the fertile wilderness, sink a well somewhere that the engine can halt to drink, and a shanty, weather-beaten as a wasp's nest, will come down in a few days over the roll of the prairie, and treat itself to some new clapboards and a coat of paint white as a sepulchre, and there it will stand close beside the track to see the cars go by.

Soon, another will creep up from the bushy run and range itself alongside, and ten to one that it will shout at you in monstrous pica lettered along its whole front, METROPOLITAN HOTEL! You have always observed that the smaller the inn the bigger the title, much after the fashion of the naturalists who "call names," and denominate a harmless little chimney-swallow an Hirundo Pelasgia! Then more houses, a church with a chuckle-headed belfry, a school-house, a· store, all white as this week's washing. Then one money-purse of a mail-bag will be thrown off from a passing train upon the depot platform, and another handed on as easily as a woman's work-pocket.

The village is christened Athens, it has a P.M., and when a little village grows to have a P.M., it is getting pretty well along towards A.M. Day has fairly broke. Untilled breadths of prairie round about begin to show scars. The plow is busy. They set out trees, and settle a minister and hire a schoolma'am. They fit up a hall over a store, and call it Apollo. A man comes along with a composing-stick in his pocket and starts a newspaper. It is the *Clarion.* The editor thanks one man for a pumpkin and measures it. He confesses to a turkey and acknowledges the corn. He says he is amazed at the great West. A young lawyer gets off the cars, and immediately another. A solitary lawyer is useless. What would Robinson Crusoe have done had he been an attorney? His story would have been *brief*, and no red tape to tie it with. No, a couple of lawyers are like two halves of a pair of shears. You need them both for the cutting purposes of the legal instrument. Two doctors are there already. Then an artist arrives with his house on wheels, and backs it upon a vacant lot next to the " Metropolitan," and there it is, with a monstrous lobster - like eye in the top, and the girls and their " fellows " come in from around about to be taken — come in their best; great healthy girls, wearing three or four dresses apiece, each shorter than the other, and all flounced, or fluted, or something.

The railway has brought the fashions. It also brought that Chinese abomination, a gong. The " Metropolitan " has one, and it frightened an innocent man into running away with a span of horses, and they never got him. It also threw a feeble woman into convulsions who had been reading Gordon's Adventures in Africa—not the "lord" of that ilk. She either thought it was a lion or she was in Africa, but she never explained. The rival hotel, called " The Orient," because it is located in the Occident, and completed yesterday, has not attained to gongs. It only rings a bell.

A barber arrives. His fathers, some of them, were from the coast of Guinea. He is table-waiter at the Metropolitan. Likewise an artist on leather, with dramatic tendencies, for he strikes an attitude and cries, "What boots it!" and then laughs like a general alarm in a poultry-yard. He is ostler at the Metropolitan, also porter. He punishes a fiddle for the dancers at the Apollo. He shaves.

The Methodists came first. They have a choir with a pitch-pipe to it. Next the Baptists, with a melodeon. They both will try for an organ next year. THE EXAMINER has a club bigger than can be cut anywhere within four miles of Athens.

And this Athens is as much the product of the locomotive as a puff of steam. It made things possible. The next thing the prince of modern genii does, is to bolt the track without tumbling into the ditch. It goes across-lots to some sleepy little ante-railroad Corners, that was the county-seat aforetime, and trails the Court-house, by a figure of speech, back to Athens, and it becomes the Capital! All the boys are aching to do something whereby they may get into the new jail. At last the Sheriff catches a rogue and locks him up, and the boys are satisfied. The thin lawyer with the thin tin sign becomes Judge, and also fatter. It was a graveyard they had over at the Corners, a straggling place where people lay down wherever they pleased, and nobody said a word. Things are not thus in

Athens. They have laid out a—cemetery, with some pretension to beauty, and have traced it off with paths and avenues like the lines upon the palm of a hand. They also have a hearse. So has the Corners, but then Athens has *plumes,* when people die that can · afford it.

There are a briskness of step and a precision of speech about the people of a railway creation that you never find in a town that is only accessible to a stage-driver, and where they go sauntering about like a Connecticut one-horse chaise. There it is always three o'clock till it is four. In Athens never. From the depot with its time-table to the dusky factotum of the "Metropolitan," everybody carries a watch. He compares it with the standard at the depot once a day. He consults it upon all possible occasions. If you begin to preach, he times you from the text. If you marry him to somebody, he whips out his repeater, and sees just how long you were about it. The second-hand, so useless in a lazy old town, is magnified in importance to a crowbar. You ask him the time, and he tells you "Number Six, due here at two o'clock and one minute, has just gone. I'm thirty seconds slow. It's two o'clock and four minutes!" And there you have the time almost accurate enough for an astronomer. The locomotive is an accomplished educator. It teaches everybody that virtue of princes we call punctuality. It waits for nobody. It demonstrates what a useful creature a minute is in the economy of things.

The West is full of Athenses that were. They have grown greater and better. They star the prairies as constellations the heavens. They have grown more modest and less pretentious with time. Villages, like girls, have "a hateful age." There is a period, too, in the life of villages, when they resemble that red-nightcapped carpenter, the woodpecker — they are biggest when first hatched.

CHAPTER XXI.

A CABOOSE RIDE.

HAS it ever happened to you to be left somewhere, and nothing to get away upon but a
freight train? And did the train happen to be
running on an Express train's time, and did you
make the flitting in the night? If "yes," you
remember it. The writer was at Friendship, in
the State of New York. It adjoins the town of
Amity, whose post-office ought to be Fraternity.
What a dreadful thing this "calling names" has
become! Down that same Erie Road is Scio,
and not a man of them can tell where Homer
was buried. Then we have Cuba and Castile,
and nothing Spanish or Castilian in either of
them, except the Castile *soap* at the druggist's.
Avon, without Shakspeare; Caledonia, and nobody to bless the Duke of Argyle for a scratch-
ing-post; Warsaw, that Campbell does not sing
of in his "Pleasures of Hope;" Ararat, and no
sign of Noah's ark; Waterloo, that Bonaparte

never lost; Cato, Ovid, Camillus, Marcellus, and all the rest of them.

To return to the freight train: You climb aboard, and entering the caboose sit down before you mean to, the thing giving a plunge just before you are ready. Four or five men are disposed about the car. They are drovers. You think you have blundered into a barnyard. Those men have their outdoor voices with them. Their frequent conversations with herds have made them boisterous and breezy as the month of March. The society of cattle is not always refining, especially of cattle to kill. You don't see anybody reading poetry. The stove burns wood, and not coal, but the car is smutty for all that. They use many good words, but they don't seem to understand the *arrangement* of them. You begin to be sorry you did not tarry at Jericho for the passenger train. But these men are kind-hearted. One of them moves along and lets you sit within six inches of the stove that, unless like a blackberry, it is red when it is green, must be dead ripe.

The car is a short caboose, fashioned like a small, ill-shaped back kitchen, and it has no more wheels than a one-horse wagon, which gives it an uneasy and suggestive way on the track. A brakeman sits with his head swung out at a window. The conductor sits with his watch in

his hand. Nobody has any business there at all.
The engineer is doing his best to make a distant station, and get upon the side-track before
the Express wants the road. You find this out
by degrees. It makes you feel light, but not
airy. The kitchen rocks like a cradle for a dozen
rods, and then jounces the light out and the
water-barrel over and your hat off, and the stove
rattles like a smithy in a driving time. Then
it gathers itself up like a salient goat, and
bounces against the bumper of the next car and
something snaps. No matter.

The train swings around a curve, and you feel
as u did years ago when you were the last
boy on the string in the game of "snap the
whip." You steady your lower jaw a little, and
ask the conductor if he is going to stop before
he stops for good, to-wit: meets the Express, and
he says, "Genesee!" It occurs to you that he
has mentioned the very place you are bound for,
though you never heard of it before. The conductor informs you it is safe to bet we are "just
dusting," and you believe him — the *only* safe
thing about the train. It is thirty miles an hour.
Another head is hung out of a window, and you
think you'll try to count fence-posts. It does n't
happen to be a fence, but a stockade; and as
for telegraph-poles, you have seldom observed
them thicker to the mile. You look forward, and

see lights down the track. Drawing in like a
turtle, you tell the conductor. " What is it,
Joe ? " and the brakeman replies " Nothin'."
The conductor puts his watch to his ear. Has
it stopped ? With rattle and roar the engineer
keeps launching the train into the midnight. A
shrill shriek of the locomotive whistles you up,
and you are on your feet like a cat. The
brakeman runs up his little iron ladder, the speed
slackens, the train comes to a dead halt. It is
Genesee, and one grateful passenger leaves that
frantic caboose, to set foot in it, as he fervently
prays, " nevermore."

20

CHAPTER XXII.

HATCHING OUT A WOMAN.

WHEN the necromancer turns farmer, sows a few kernels of wheat in a little tin-box of earth, claps on the cover, sends a few sparks of electricity through it, whips off the lid and shows you the green blades an inch and a half long, in a minute and a half, it is a phenomenon, but not a miracle. You can see something quite as marvelous in the World on Wheels any day. Enter a well-filled car in " the wee small hours ayont the twal." The light is dim but not religious with the uncertain glimmer of candles or the smoky flare of kerosene, which ought to be banished from every civilized and Christian road. The seats are heaped with shapeless piles of clothes. Folks are shut up like jack-knives or bagged like game. Here and there a head is visible, swaying about when there is n't any wind, as if everything had "lodged" except a bearded stalk now and then. By-and-by the gray, cold, unspeculative dawn begins to show at the East windows, and there is a stir among the bundles. A man with hair over his front like a Shetland pony's mane emerges from a blanket. A boy with the head of a distaff changes ends. A girl blossoms out in the next seat.

But there is one large heap of clothes that you watch, and they are good ones. A dainty hat with a feather in it swings from the rack above by one string. A muff like a well-to-do cat reposes in the wire manger. The bundle appears to be composed of cloaks, shawls, and a lap-robe. It is *shaped* like an egg, and it *is* an egg. First one shawl gives a little lift, then another. There is a slight surge of a cloak. Off goes a shawl. A snug gaiter with a foot in it emerges at one end, and a disheveled head at the other. Forth comes a hand, and at last the chrysalis is rent, and the occupant is hatched out before your eyes. But it is anything but a butterfly. It is a crumpled, drowsy piece of womanhood, who slept in her head but not in her hair.

The trying, pitiless light of early morning plays upon her terrifically, and she knows it. It amuses you to watch her under your eyelids. She brings forth from her reticule a liver-shaped device, and she hangs it on behind, like the fender of a canal-boat, just over her combativeness and philo-progenitiveness, and what not. Then she arranges and sorts out curls and ringlets for different organs. You ought to see that head. It grows like a soap-bubble. She claps a love of a friz on her self-esteem, which allies her to angels; a coil of a curl upon her firmness, which brings her, sometimes, within neighborly distance of donkeys; she borders her brow with ringlets, trails a braid about her inhabitiveness and constructiveness, touches up the tress on her veneration, and the head is artistically complete. She washes her face with a handkerchief, rights her collar, shakes out the creases, tosses the little hat upon the top of all things, and is ready for breakfast. Who talks of necromantic *wheat*, when here is a human *flower* hatched from an awkward bundle in less than thirty minutes!

When you take a train with a *harem* in it— I use the word in its originally clean sense— and you have no *personal* interest in the harem, you are apt to fare badly. The train is meant where the women are sorted out for one car, and what is left is just turned into another. It is a vicious fashion, and fosters the art of lying. There goes a young man at the heels of a lady whom he never saw before, or spoke to in his life, and he is carrying a spick-and-span new bandbox. My word for it, it is as empty as a church contribution-box on Saturday afternoon. He bought that box for precisely that emergency. The lady ascends the platform. So does the bandbox. The brakeman opens the door, and the young man slips in unquestioned, and secures a comfortable seat. He means to study for the ministry, and he has been lying by bandbox !

There is another man. He appears to be a good man. You are sure he is, and he stands where the brakeman can see him, and touches his hat to a window of the harem where nobody is sitting, and then, with a little smiling affectionate haste, he skips up the steps and says, " Please let me in a minute ! " and in he goes. That unfortunate man never beheld a face in that car in all his life. The more you think of it the more vicious the fashion seems. It does not benefit the ribbons, and is a positive damage to the whiskers. Pen men up together, and if they do not act like cattle it will be in spite of the pen ! Women sprinkled through the cars keep the train upon its honor, if not upon the track, and elevate the lumbering thing from a common carrier to an educator.

Flying bedrooms are among the crowning achievements of railway travel. They are gorgeous. They remind you — the most of them — of the Hall of Representatives at Washington, which in its turn suggests a Chinese pagoda. They are luxuries. If you do n't mind plunging endwards through your dreams at forty miles an hour ; and if you do n't care whom you sleep

with; and if you never catch cold; and if you
have no "reasonable doubt" as to getting out,
provided the bed-room is mistaken for a dice-box,
some night, and you are sure you will not come
within an ace of throwing the deuce, there is
nothing like them. Snores in many languages are
let loose upon you, and feet from many boots.
The porter has an appetite for boots. He sits
up at night to get yours, no matter where you
put them, and there he is in the morning, the
boots in one hand and nothing in the other. It
is pleasant, also, to have the drapery of your
couch whisked one side every few minutes, just as
you have dropped off into a doze, and a strange
hand passed over your face, by somebody blun-
dering about in quest of his berth.

Flying drawing-rooms *deserve* what winged bedrooms *need* — unmitigated praise. The clank of
wheels is shut out. You exult to the angles of
your elbows, because there is room for them.
You can go about in your revolving chair like
a shingle chanticleer upon a barn - ridge. You
read quietly, write comfortably, converse easily.
It is home adrift.

CHAPTER XXIII.

A FLANK MOVEMENT.

IN war and peace all people are afraid of a flank movement. General Sherman, though he never quite found out what newspapers are for, *did* discover that the Federal strength was in the enemy's flanks. In other words, if the Confederate army had been finished off prematurely like a pictorial cherub, he would have had nothing to punish. It is said to be a dreadful strain upon a man's muscles to kick at nothing! In a railway car a man is apt to be flanked by somebody—a small army of observation in the rear.

Take a man who has a fine sense of feeling all over, and put two women behind him—one woman thus located is comparatively harmless, but two are a terror, for they can talk about you!—and he begins to wonder if his collar is clean behind, and how he looks just back of his ears, and whether a stray string, or something, may not be sticking up above his coat, though he cannot remember that he ever had anything there to be *tied*. Then he tries to remember whether he brushed his hair neatly behind, in his haste this morning, lest he should be behind himself. Just at that minute there is a coincidence; a little laugh from the ladies on the next seat, and footsteps on the rim of his ear! It is mid-winter, and it cannot be a fly. If he were only sure it was a tarantula, he would be happy. They laugh again, and again that small promenader. He *knows* his head harbors nothing but ideas, and yet a trespasser may have come from foreign pastures, for all that. He wishes he knew—that he could see himself as " ithers see" him at that particular minute.

Can it possibly be of the race that Burns discovered upon the woman's Sunday bonnet? He dares not put his hand up, lest they should observe it. He feels his ears grow red and warm. He wishes they would get hot enough to scorch that creature's feet. Still those small footsteps. He has heard, in his time, the tramp of armed men. It was sublimer, but not half so terrible. Again that little laugh behind him, and rising in his desperation he goes to the rear of the car, claps his hand to the burning ear, and secures a single hair like a bit of a watch-spring, that had coiled on the rim of the human sea-shell, and counterfeited feet that his fancy built upon, as Agassiz built two-story monsters out of a rafter or a rib that somebody exhumed and sent to him. And those ladies had never seen him at all!

If a man could always have the world in his front, courage would not be much of a virtue, if it *ever* is. There are a great many worthless things passed about as genuine. Now, that little Spartan scamp who stole the fox, hid it under his robe, and let the creature relieve him of his liver rather than be found out and lose the plunder, is handed about with a label to him, as a sort of pocket-model of fortitude. I dug it out of Greek when I was a boy, and was taught it was worth finding. Why, he was nothing but a miserable little thief, that could n't speak a word of English! So, if courage is a virtue, the brave little wren carries more virtue to the ounce than anything going. The writer knows a public speaker who trembles as did the king who saw something written on the wall, if he is compelled to pass through the body of the house to reach the platform, and yet always faces the audience with perfect self-possession. He has been known to flounder through an unbroken snow-drift, and climb in by a window, simply to avoid the flank movement that took all his courage out of him. When you see a man turn a cold shoulder to a chilling wind instead of squarely facing it, you may count him among the victims of rheumatism, and not among the philosophers.

21*

CHAPTER XXIV.

LIGHT AND SHADE.

THE saddest train upon which the writer ever took passage was the Hospital Train, with its maimed and mangled burden, that ran from the still, white tents of Stevenson, Ala., to Nashville, Tenn., just after the battle of Chickamauga. There was no lack of ventilation, for some of the cars were platforms — the kind that make Martyrs, but not Presidents. Not much finish in precious woods anywhere that you could see. It rained heavily and persistently through the twelve hour trip, and there the wounded lay strewn about on the platforms, and packed away in the box-cars. But you heard less complaint than is made any day on a palace-train because one refractory rose-leaf is crumpled. The suffering was silent, and all the more terrible because it was so. The stricken boys had started for home, and there was a strange, ghastly cheerfulness upon their faces, that was sadder than sadness. They

talked about "God's country," whither they were
bound, till your heart ached to think how many
of them would find "God's acre" before they
reached the blessed North.

The bearing of that wounded brigade was wonderfully glorified with the grace of patience. It
taught you what splendid stuff human nature is
made of. They tell about men of iron, and
nerves of steel, and look as if they thought they
had said something — as if there were anything
quite so good to make a man of as the flesh
that can quiver and the nerve that can twinge.
Those cars on that Chattanooga Road were bad
enough, though the reader cannot get the idea
unless he amuses himself by riding upon a lively
trip-hammer; but of all wheeled contrivances,
the ambulance that was used in the late war is
the most spiteful. You would naturally think it
"an invention of the enemy"—that he had devised it for the special purpose of finishing the
people he had not quite killed with gunpowder.
The jolty, jerky thing, with wolf-trap springs that
snap at every inequality in the road, and send
waves of pain through the shattered frames of
its occupants, is, for a merciful device, certainly
the most cruel. Be our prayer, that neither
hospital train nor ambulance will be needed evermore in all the land!

Did you ever see troops of young swallows peppering the southern slope of a broad-roofed barn, just as they are making ready to leave for a sunnier clime? What confusion of happy tongues, what half-human chatter and frolic. If you would see the same picture later in the season, after the swallows are all gone, just board a passenger train in December upon a road lined with schools for girls, like the Chicago and Milwaukee, when the flocks are let loose and bound home for the holidays. The birds are gayer and brighter, and worth a gallon of swallows every one of them, no matter whether swallows are higher than sparrows or not—half a farthing apiece—but they recall the picture on the barn-slope, till the girls and the birds seem to be twittering over the same dish of joyous expec- tation.

You had left Milwaukee a little dull and a trifle surly, but as the train halts along at those beautiful villages where the dove-cotes are, and the merry creatures throng aboard, and captivate you and take the train, and fill it with laughter and ribbons, and jaunty little hats about as big as the palm of your hand, and sit down three in a seat, when their flounces will let them, and talk all at once and all the time, then you, too, brighten up and grow human, and wish you were a boy or a girl again, so that you could

see things rose-colored, and think it blessing
enough to live, and be happy without a plan.
Whoever says gravely to himself, "I am going
to be happy to-day," is pretty sure to have a
sober-sided time of it. I do not think anybody
can *toe* happiness, as the children used to toe a
crack when they stood up to spell. A great
deal of the commodity comes to a man when he
is not looking for it, just as a side-glance sometimes reveals a star that the astronomer had
been vainly seeking with the direct gaze.

The Lord has arranged things wisely for our
mere physical delight. He has not planted all
the violets in the world in one place, neither
has He fenced in the roses between particular
lines and parallels of latitude and longitude, nor
fashioned them to grow up close under our noses.
But we go carelessly along, and we get a whiff
of the violets down there in the grass, and the
lilacs over yonder in the yard, and the roses in
the fence corner, and they all go to make up the
fragrance and the beauty of the day, though we
had not been looking for any of them. It is the
indirect ray from everything, whether it be the
sun or the drop of dew, that unravels and makes
visible the beauty of the world.

There is a great deal said about *spheres*. A
planetary stranger would think that about half
the world were engaged in getting a lesson in

Spherical Trigonometry — man's sphere and woman's sphere. Most of the unhappiness, uneasiness, and tendency to bolt spheres, is due to an impression many people unconsciously entertain, that the Lord did not understand His business when He made the Gardener and his wife — that he could have made a better job of it. Take an open-browed, clean-hearted girl, blessed with a fair share of beauty of some kind, and then make her believe that she is about the neatest piece of work the Lord ever made, and *keep* her believing so, and you will have a woman by-and-by, if heaven does n't want her before, who will never trouble herself much about spheres and tangents, or any other problems of Social Geometry, but will just brighten and sweeten the world all the days of her life.

The day those school-girls came into the car there was a sour-visaged man in it whom you had been watching. His features were all huddled together — he had done it himself — his eyes, nose, mouth and chin all puckered to a focus of chronic anxiety. He looked as if he had been getting those features all ready to be poured through a tunnel into a vinegar-barrel. You were curious to observe the effect of the merry inroad upon him. At first not a movement. He seemed as sulphuric as ever. Some of the girls threw little smiles his way, though not at him, and some of them *hit* him, and he began to watch them. They were too many for him, and he concluded he would n't run into the vinegar-barrel just yet.

It was curious to see that small mass-meeting of features break up and distribute themselves around his face, each in its place, until his countenance got about as broad as a sun - dial, and about as bright as the dial does when the sun shines on it. He had been thinking for a long time that he needed medicine of some kind. As he would have worded it himself, " he felt a good eel out of kilter," but it was young folks he needed all the while, and nothing at all that a druggist could sell him.

CHAPTER XXV.

PRECIOUS CARGOES.

THE richest cargo in the world is a cargo of TIME, and the locomotive was made to draw it. Yesterday I saw a man who tugged his household goods and gods from East to West in thirty days. To be sure, the roads had three dimensions, length, breath and — *thickness;* — who ever knew a migrant to flit in pleasant weather? — but he drove early and late, and tired out the family dog and took him aboard — the dog that had developed his muscles in digging out woodchucks and shaking pole - cats to pieces in the Catskills. He has made that journey since in thirty hours, and his account between the old time and the new stands 1 : 24 — a pretty formidable balance when the commodity is a thing so precious as time.

Take that piece of animated nature called the commercial traveler, who slings his little knapsack under his left shoulder-blade and says, " the world is mine oyster ! " He is as much a pro-

duct of the lócomotive as a puff of steam. He is
a wholesale store in a pair of boots. The great
house in New York, Chicago, Cincinnati, is trundled about the world by sample, and he girds up
his loins and keeps it company. The engine has
made him possible. He is about as wonderful as
the Arabian Genius that came out of the little
bottle and clouded all the land. Let us say he
travels fifteen thousand miles a year; that he
keeps upon the track ten years without breaking his neck; that he begins his commercial
raids at the age of twenty-two, unships his little
knapsack, buys out the wholesale house he
"represented," and retires from the road at
thirty-two, thus making a beginning so noble
that it fairly laps over upon the ending.

Now, could you set back his almanac for him
about a generation, a couple of hundred years
would be little enough to accomplish the work,
and he must bequeath the unfinished business
to his great-grandson—a legacy from his dead and
gone ancestor. Here he is now, with the work
done, all the silver on his dining-table, and not
a thread of it in his hair! Those witches and
wizards of locomotives have drawn a cargo of
more than two centuries about the world for
him, upon which *he* could draw at will, and his
draft was honored every time. They have made
his days "long in the land," no matter what

23

he thought of his father; made a young Methuselah of him, two hundred and fifty years old if a day, and the grasshopper not a grain heavier.

The modern cars have taken aboard what was little thought of in the early history of locomotives — *breathing* material. Ventilation has by no means attained perfection, but remember the low, narrow boxes, almost as close as mortality's "long home," that they used to call coaches, in which people made sardines of themselves, and caught colds and influenzas and asthmas and catarrhs and other musical instruments, and you will not feel like being very querulous over the discomforts of modern locomotion. That ancient fashion — it was the best the stupid old world knew — of boxing a man up in cars full of nitrogen, was an abomination to chemistry and comfort. A stove in the center, a sort of altar for the rendering of unseemly offerings that Sir Walter Raleigh is said to be answerable for, used to form a torrid zone about eight feet broad, subdued into a pair of temperates, and eked out at the ends with a couple of frigids, and there you have the climate of the old railroads. Then, what with those who broke fast on bolognas and the blessed vegetable that used to keep the girls of Weathersfield a-crying, you had all the odors of Cologne *except* cologne.

Did you ever watch a kitten under a receiver when the air-pump began to rob her of her breathing material?—the signs of distress, the furry sides working like a busy bellows, the be- wildered looking about for help? If it was a talented kitten, perhaps she discovered the fatal orifice in the brazen floor whence her life was escaping, and clapped her paw upon it, as cats have done before now, and so stopped the rob- bery and won respect and saved her life. This time the victim is not a cat but a king, to-wit, one of the American sovereigns, secured in an old-time car, with nothing aboard to make breath of. It is curious to see how he degenerates by a series of melancholy transitions into a miserable vegetable. You put him into the car brisk and bright as nature will let him be. The sixth hour he grows irritable; the tenth, dull. His fancy leaves him in the fifteenth. He begins to think how far it is to dinner, and how much he will eat, for he is just passing through the brute region, on his way from humanity down to vege- tation, where his epitaph might be, "gone to grass." The eighteenth hour he is surly; the twentieth, dumb. The twenty-fourth "does" for him and the metamorphosis is complete, the necromantic experiment is over. He cannot re- member who wrote Milton's "Paradise Lost." He forgets the name of the principal character in Hamlet. He runs up a few rounds of the multiplication table just to see if they are all there. He ceases to think at all, looks steadily out of the window and sees nothing. He ceases to count anything in the census. He is not so much as Nebuchadnezzar. He is grass.

But "all things have become new." What speed in the engine; what priceless cargoes of time and oxygen upon the train; how fast and long we live in a little while! Let us be glad. Uneasy people sometimes wish they had been born in the days of Alexander, or Moses, or Methuselah, or somebody who looms up gigantically in the mists of history. It is better to live in the days of the Steam-engine. It has conquered more worlds than Alexander, traversed vaster wildernesses than the Israelite, and reclaimed them as it went; and behold, by the power of the Engine we live to be hundreds of years old, and never give it a thought!

Studying life on the railroad train and looking into a kaleidoscope are somewhat alike. You cannot exhaust the figures in the one, and almost every turn of the wheels brings up a new and curious combination in the other. And so I find myself wondering why I omitted this, forgot that, and ever thought I could possibly be content with the few chance glimpses at thirty miles an hour that are here recorded.

The Engineer has rung the bell, the Conductor has pulled the cord, the Passenger Train has gone. There is nothing now to be done except to ship by a dull freight train a little heavy

BAGGAGE

CHAPTER I.

MY STARRY DAYS.

THERE are some stars to which, in my boy-hood, I was wont to lay special claim. Perhaps everybody is. I never thought of their being out of the jurisdiction of the State of New York, where I first began to "see stars," not meaning those early experiments upon the glare ice of Leonard's Pond, when my heels went up like Mercury's, and my head went down like the flint-lock of an old Queen's arm. One large ripe star used to tremble just over the edge of Clinton's Woods — I loved to fancy it would lodge some-time, and I would go a-nutting for worlds as I did for beech-nuts — a star with such a warm and human sort of light, so like an earthly fire-side somewhere, with the door open, that it always inspired a home feeling, and I counted it as much among the belongings of that particular landscape as the daisies in the pasture, and not more than a breath or two farther off.

I have heard since that it has charmed no end of poets to write verses to it that never were sent; that it is called Venus, when it deserves an honest womanly name.—Mary or Rachel, Ruth or Eve. Is it not strange that we christen a great beautiful world as we would not dare name anybody's daughter, unless her mother had an extra pair of feet in daily use, or her father were content to be called "Towzer"—at least now that the turbaned "aunty," who opened her mouth like a piano and laughed clear across the plantation, has been "amended" and counted in among the souls to be saved.

If the heathen began the nomenclature of the skies, pray let it be ended by Christians. There are no Alexanders about, to be crying for new worlds. They are glittering into the field of view every night or two, and the business of naming goes on after the fashion of dead and dusty idolaters. Had Adam made such work "calling names" when the Lord bade him, he would have been sent down on his knees there in Eden to weed onions unto tears and repentance. Let our star-finders give them a hint—those keen fellows who shall, by-and-by, roll that date of theirs, *Anno Domini* 3,000, over and over like a school of dolphins—that *we*, at least, have abandoned Latin and Greek gods; that our poultry are quite safe for all anybody in America, ·be he fool or philosopher, ordering a cock served up to Æsculapius.

But if ever anything thoroughly belonged to the owner, the heavenly Dipper — that magnificent utensil knobbed at the angles and riveted along the handle with seven stars—belonged to me. I should have clutched it long ago if, like the dagger of Shakespeare's man, it had only hung " the handle toward my hand;" as much household ware as its humble cousin forty times removed, that hung by a little chain beside the well. From that celestial dipper — or so I thought — the dews were poured out gently on the summer world. It was the only thing about the house perfectly safe from thieves and rust; for was it not of a truth a treasure laid up in heaven? And how sadly right I was; for there, only last night, blazed the Dipper as if it were fire-new, while the ·home of my boyhood has faded out like a dream and vanished away.

There was yet another trinket of domesticated heaven, if I may say so. No matter what name the Chaldeans called it by, to me it will always be the star in the well. A gray sweep swayed up above that well like an acute accent; and in its round liquid disc, that gave me glance for

23

glance, I used to see sometimes the double of a star straight from the top of heaven. It was plainer than any pearl that "ever lay under Oman's green water." They that drank at that well in the old days, long ago sat down by the river of crystal in the Kingdom of Life, but its dark disc, like a strange unwinking eye, still watches the zenith from its depths, and sometimes a star is let down into it till it kindles as if lighted by a thought.

That handful of household stars is a part of my heritage. No matter how dim the night, how disastered the sky, I close my eyes and they yet rise strangely beautiful and shine across the cloudy world even as they always shone since their illustrious kindred began to sing together. The prayer of the athletic savage was "for light." But our terrestrial day is only a veil thick-woven of sunbeam warp and woof. The dewy hand of Night withdraws it, and lo! the heavens are all abroad! Let Ajax mend his prayer, and let the burden be for calm unclouded night.

But there is another constellation not less precious than my sidereal possessions — a cluster of day-stars as resplendent as if they were called Arcturus every one. They shine with a warm and genial ray — undimmed, thank God! by any care or cloud. Time is not, as most men think, a natural product. It is only fragments of duration fashioned into shape. The whirling worlds of God are so much burnished machinery for making times and seasons. They ripple the everlasting current of white and dumb duration. It swells in ages, undulates in years; and all along the ceaseless solemn flow, sparkle like syllables of song the days of all our lives. The tumbling planets end their work, and man's begins. Whoever stamps the image and superscription of a worthy deed, a sterling truth, a splendid fact, upon a day, has hallowed and brightened it evermore. The day a man is born who rallies the sluggish race and puts it on its honor for all time, stands out from the rank and file of the dull almanac and halts you like a sentinel. The day a man is dead who gave some *other* day a might and meaning it never had before, is strewn with immortelles and borne abreast with marching ages.

Take a twenty-fifth of January, one hundred and eleven years ago — standing there in its place as plain as yesterday, illuminated all over, like an old saint's legend, with Scottish song that comes to a man like the beat of his heart,— and tell me if you think it worth while for anybody to be born on that recurring day with any hope of wresting it from " Robert Burns, Poet"? True, the Ettrick Shepherd saw the light on a twenty-fifth, but the best we can do for him is to let his "Skylark" warble up to the top of the wintry morning if it can.

The Man of Mount Vernon endowed February, that cheapest of the months, with a twenty-second it never owned before; took what had been a blank white leaf between a brace of nights, so bent back upon it the radiant truth of all his life, that, independent of the sun, it shines right on — the radiant truth that the man of truest symmetry is the man of truest power.

And what more can any one do for that seventh of February than he did to be born in it, whom Dombey shall lead gently by the hand far down another age, for whom Little Nell shall plead with a forgetful world, and who left us the voice of Tiny Tim for a perpetual benediction — "God bless us, Every one!"

The old-time Fourth.

I WOULD not give much for the American who has nowhere in the year a day domed like a tower and filled with a chime of bells. Now, the FOURTH OF JULY is one of my days with stars in it, and bells withal, that shine and ring and roar out of my childhood with an eloquence that always sets the heart pounding with the concussion of the anvil and the feet keeping step to the frolic of Yankee Doodle. It lights up the time when you could stand upright under life's Eastern eaves; when day broke in the thunder of a six-pounder, and the sun came up to the clangor of the village bell, and the bare and barkless spar they had raised and planted the night before, budded like Aaron's rod, and blossomed out with the broad field of stars.

On comes the drum-major, now with "eyes to the front all," and now facing the music with backward step, his arms swaying up and down, the horizontal baton grasped firmly in his hands, as if he were working the band with a *brake*, and playing streams of martial melody on mankind. Then the snarl of the snare-drums, all careened for punishment like refractory boys of the old-fashioned stripe, and the growl of the big bass brother at their heels, and the fifes warbling up and down in the grumble and roar, possessed and summoned up my soul—shall I say it and give thanks?—possess and summon up my soul to-day. Then came the flag with an eagle on it, and two spontoons beside it to pierce that eagle's enemies. Then the patriots of the Revolution, who remembered when there was no such thing as a Fourth of July with a big F; old, smoky fellows, two or three, with eagles in their eyes—old fellows gnarled like the hemlock, but honored like the pine, that had smelled powder at Bennington; and the orator of the day with an eagle in his eye; and the clergyman who had prayed a short prayer and fired a long gun at Yorktown or somewhere, with an eagle in *his* eye.

Then, to the tune of " Bonaparte crossing the Rhine," out stepped the white-legged infantry, with breasts and backs of blue, each with an eagle sewed upon a bright tin plate, all garnished round with stars and fastened to his hat, and that eagle's royal tail feathering out at the top the while, to plume him up like Henry of Navarre.

Then came the riflemen in green frock-coats and caps befringed, and horns slung at their sides, that once were tossed defiant upon a shaggy head that might have answered back the bulls of Bashan, and had, for anything you know, an eagle in *its* eye; and on they went, their rifles lightly borne to the order of " *Trail*——ARMS!" Ah, it was " the hunters of Kentucky" all over again. It was the whole Boone family in the flesh. It was an apparition of the dark and bloody ground.

Then, with the warble of bugle and much clatter, clang and ring of hoofs and spurs and scabbards, the old-fashioned troopers rode by with eagles in *their* eyes; their holsters, small packages of thunder and lightning, at the saddle-bow; their shiny cylinders of portmanteaus snugly strapped behind; the terrible frown of a bear-

skin cap lowering on every brow, its jaunty
feather, tipped with emblematic blood, springing
out of the fur like the blossom of a magnified
and glorified bull-thistle — and the flare of the
red-coats set the scene and your heart on fire
together!

Then came the citizens by twos, as the pairs
went into the ark, and the girls in white frocks
with sashes and ribbons of blue, as if they had
just torn out of heaven and brought away with
them some fragments of azure for token; but
there are no eagles any more in the line — only
white doves and angels unfallen. Then the mouth
of the orator was opened — a coop of rhetorical
eagles, and they flew abroad and swooped down
upon our feelings and bore them aloft triumphant,
and perched upon our souls and made eyries in
our lofty hearts, and we were better and braver
for it all. Then came the dinner in a "bower"
— have you quite forgotten the dining-hall of green
branches? — with such dainty roasters as the
Gentle Elia would have wept over and then de-
voured, and toasts that foamed over the tops of
the goblets and set themselves aright in the
cups; and a flight of hurrahs went up with the
eagles — and the day was done.

Do you think I would exchange that dear
absurd old day for "the pomp and circumstance"
of any later pageant? A Fourth-of-Julyism has

somehow become an object of contempt. People tell us, but not always in good English, that speeches are idle, because they have heard that silence is golden, and, like the green spectacles of Moses and the talk of the rascal in the Vicar of Wakefield, should be labeled "*fudge.*" As if it was not an *idea* clothed in a snug jacket of words, and not a deed at all, that first gave the Fourth of July a meaning and a gift to mankind! As if the elder Adams' recipe to pickle the day—I write with no irreverence—to pickle the day in "villainous saltpetre" would not be sure to keep it! As if the roar of artillery—thank God for the blank cartridges of Independence!—were anything more than that eloquent whisper uttered under the shadow of King's Mountain in the old North State, "these colonies are, and of right ought to be, free," translated into the dialect of gunpowder! Shine on, starry day of my boyhood! Thy thunders, thy eagles, and thy memories, be they blessed forever!

Thanksgiving.

I am sorry for the man—especially the woman —who has nowhere a day or two touched with some tender grace; a day of which, travel fast and far as he may, he is never out of sight; that warms his heart for him, makes him gentler, purer, younger than before, more like a woman and just as much of a man. Everywhere else in Christendom the year has three hundred and sixty-five days, but in America it has a day of grace, and as much a New England product as Joel Barlow or Indian corn: for we count three hundred and sixty-five days and THANKS-GIVING.

As everybody knows, the day was the most blessed of blunders. Those single-minded, grand old fellows—old when they were young—that drifted across the sea in the cup of a Flower like a parcel of bees, bringing, some of them, their stings with them, and from whose rude beginnings this broad continent now hums like a hive in June, had garnered their corn, and tugged up their back-logs, and kicked the light snow of "squaw winter" from their Spanish-leather boots, and hung up their tall hats on the pegs behind the door, and picked their flints for such game as red Indian and black bear, and spread open their Bibles, and made ready for a sojourn before the fire; then came one of the American savages they never shot at—to-wit: Indian Summer.

> For past the yellow regiments of corn
> There came an Indian maiden, autumn-born ;
> And June returned and held her by the hand,
> And led Time's smiling Ruth through all the land,

24*

So they made ready for a second planting right
away, and declared it a goodly land, where a
very thin slice of autumn was sandwiched between two summers, and decreed a Thanksgiving,
and called the neighbors together, and lifted up
their voices and sang some such quaint song as—

> " Ye monsters of the bubbling deep,
>   Your Maker's praises spout ;
> Up from your sands, ye codlings, peep,
>   And wag your tails about ! "

and clasped each other's hands, and feasted
abundantly, and took " a cup of kindness," and
grew so warm with what they had and what
they *would* have, that when Euroclydon and all
the rest of them did come, and that right early,
their gratitude never froze, but wintered it
through ; and so Thanksgiving remains even until
now.

Dear Starry Day, when three generations met
together and—not to betray confidences—"right-
eousness and peace kissed each other." What
friendships were brightened in thy fire-light !
what wrongs were roasted under thy fore-stick !
Thy turnovers are imperishable as the Pleiades. Thy chickens of the nankeen legs tucked
up in a coverlet of crust, and, brooded in the
bake-kettle by its great coal-laden cover, how
comfortable they were ! Out of the glowing

cavern of the brick oven, squatted in the wall beside the fireplace like an exaggerated cat, what gusts of fragrance from thy turkeys, breasted like dead knights in armor, " whose souls are with the saints, we trust ;" what whiffs of Indian pudding ! what blended breezes of abundance ! Thy doughnuts of orthodox twist, and tinted like cedar wood, yet heap the bright tin pans of memory. Thy mighty V's of mince pies yet slant to the angle of perfect content, and fit and fill the mouth of recollection.

Surely heart and stomach are next-door neighbors, for now, Thanksgiving, thy dear old faces smile a welcome home ; thy dear old faces, every one unchanged, undimmed, unsent away. Rouse the fire to a hearty roar of greeting ! Wheel out the great table laden like the palm of Providence. Bring forth the empty chairs. Let us " ask a blessing !" Let us give thanks !

CHRISTMAS.

METHUSELAH died pretty well along in his years of discretion, but a world at his age would hardly have been out of its swaddling bands. There is a star, less than two thousand years old, that lights a day for us, the fairest, youngest of all the spangled multitude — the very Benjamin of Heaven. The telescope of the astronomer

never summoned it.   Numbered in the celestial
census, I am sure it will not be there when the
constellations are rolled together as a scroll.   It
is immortal as the candle of the Lord.   It is the
Star in the East that lights up CHRISTMAS for
us with a wonderful radiance.

If there is ever a time in all the year when
the two worlds touch, I think it is Christmas
Eve.   What less than a first small act of faith
is that hanging a million of empty stockings by
a million pins at night, and then tumbling the
trundle-beds of Christendom with the delightful
and sleepless expectancy that they will find them
all filled in the morning?   Let a man play Saturn
and *eat* his children and be done with it; but
let him not set a dog on their angels — a cur
of a fact, that should have been born with its
nose in a muzzle, upon Santa Claus or Kriss
Kringle, and worry him out of the children's
sweet kingdom of dreams.

Whoever wants to make his children older than
any wholesome grandfather ought to be, has only
to strip the world stark naked before their faces;
bare all its exquisite mystery that keeps one pair
of burnished interrogation-points for ever dancing
in another pair of eyes, resolve the thrones and
paradises and angels they see in the plighted
clouds, into a heavy and delusive fog; and, by-
and-by, for the quicksilverish atoms of humanity

that hunt out every grain of true gold in the
rubbish of life, full of marvel and fancy and
poetry as any old ballad, he will have a row of
little desiccated, unspeculative, philosophical donkeys all draped in wet blankets.

I visited, not long ago, the house where something happened to me when I narrowly escaped
being too young to be counted, but you can never
guess what was the first thing I looked for. It
was not, as you might think, the threshold worn
smooth and beautiful by the touch of feet that
have played truant forever, nor the dear home-
room with its altar-place for beech and maple
offerings, nor yet the nook of darkness under the
stairs where goblins and ogres held sweet coun-
sel together by night.

It was only the old chimney-top my eyes first
sought, to whose rugged edges and sooty mouth-
piece a thousand boatswain winds had put their
lips and whistled up the storms for eighty years.
It was the homeliest structure that ever seemed
beautiful to anybody. Shall I tell you why?
Down that chimney the angel descended with
my first Christmas gift. What was the ladder
of Jacob to me then, has turned, at last, into a
rude unlettered monument to the dead past.

They whom I surprised with my " Merry
Christmas," in the gray of the morning, have
gone away for the everlasting holidays. The

children with whom I joined hands and hearts are — *where* are they? There are fences in the graveyard tipped with funeral urns of black. There are broken slabs of marble bearing names that have fallen out of human speech. There are hard, grim men. There are meek and sad-eyed women, full of care. *Has* the sparkle of life utterly vanished from the cup? Can the sleigh-bells' chime and the glittering nights and the laugh of young girls and the measure of old songs charm no more?

Oh, Comrades! oh, Sweethearts! Let me give you a touch of the time when happiness was the very cheapest thing in the round world: let me give you "a merry Christmas" out of the loneliness!

But children are not out of fashion, and so the world is not bankrupt. Herod — he deserves the compliment and he shall have it — Herod was nothing less than devilish shrewd when he fancied he could quench Christmas in the blood of the children; for if ever two things were made for each other, a merry child and a merry Christmas are the two.

What the poor creatures did that were born and grown before the clock of the Christian era struck "one" nobody can tell. We all *need* such days — the young that they may never grow old;

the old that they may always be young. I think it might be written among the beatitudes:

" Blessed are they whose sons are all boys and whose daughters are all girls."

It was when Cæsar Augustus decreed that "all the world" should be enrolled—an edict never to be repeated on the planet until the coming of the Seventh Angel—and everybody was on the move to report in his native city—for in that country the leap from a howling wilderness to a city was as easy as a panther's—if it did n't *howl* it had a *mayor!*

Among those who came to Bethlehem on this errand were a man and his wife from Nazareth, and, as the tavern was crowded, they went to the barn, and there the Chief of Children was born, and cradled in a manger.

And that was the first Christmas.

There were Angels without, who brought their glory with them, and they stood and sang, " Glory to God in the highest, and on earth peace to the men of good will!"

And that was the first Christmas Carol.

A few Shepherds watching their flocks not far away came just as they were, in their every-day clothes, and wondered and glorified, and were glad.

And that was the first Christmas Party.

Some travelers from the East—and wise, as you may know, by the cardinal point—were seeking the Christmas, but no one could tell them anything, till a STAR journeyed on before, and halted, like Gibeon's sun, over where the young child was—ah, always now as then, find Christmas and a child is not far off—and they unfolded their treasures, and gave him gold and frankincense and myrrh.

And that was the first Christmas Gift.

The shepherds are dead, the " wise men " are East, and the angels in Heaven. But the star and the child and the manger are everywhere. Come, let us have a frolic together! Even the turkey has a merry-thought in its breast; and are we not better than a *flock* of turkeys? Let us advertise for a good digestion and a downy pillow, and a pleasant dream and a Merry Christmas. Let us do it in these words:

> WANTED—A debtor to be forgiven.
> WANTED—A wrong to be forgotten.
> WANTED—A heart to be lightened.
> WANTED—A home to be brightened.

Wherever the Star halts, there shall be no lack of carols. Bid the singers begin! And the same old manger chorus swells sweetly again—" On earth peace to the men of good will!" Shine on, gentle Star! Merry Christmas, Good Night!

CHAPTER II.

"No. 104,163."

"THE great Mercantile Library Enterprise of San Francisco," so I read in my evening paper, "will positively distribute its prizes on the 31st of October. Tickets, five dollars in gold."

And then I turned to the glittering roll of fortunes. There they were, heaped up in an auriferous pyramid curiously balanced on its apex. At the bottom lay a poor little "$100 in gold,". not worth minding, and up swelled the shining structure, — $1,000 — $5,000 — $10,000 — $25,000 — $50,000 — until away at the top blazed clear across the column,

"$100,000 IN GOLD!"

All gold from the land of Gold, the unearthed Ophir of the Solomonic time. Everything had a bilious tint. It was as if I was seeing creation through an Oriental topaz. I felt for my ears, lest I had somehow swapped with Midas for his transmuting touch. No railway conductor was ever more clamorous for tickets than my heart was. Gold was 113 that day, so I counted out $5.65, turned it into a Post-office order, and transmitted it to the nearest agent. The ticket came, a strip of paper tawny as the Tiber, a faint reflection of " great heaps of gold," as Clarence said, but not to drown for, as Clarence *did*. It was covered with " a strange device"— the ticket was — like the handkerchief the Alpine traveler carried in his hand, who talked Latin and cried " *Excelsior!* "

To think what splendid possibilities might lurk in that oblong piece of paper was enough to take one's breath away! I said not a word to Lucy — that 's my wife — but folded it tenderly, as if it were a napkin with ten talents in it, and laid it away with a gold half dollar and a broken ring and a curl of hair and a stray pearl that had tumbled out of an old brooch, and a bit of ribbon and a faint suspicion of dead and gone fragrance — " all and singular" the con- tents of a little box that, forty years ago, would have been a " till" in the upper right-hand cor- ner of a chest of drawers, and as nearly like an old-fashioned heart as two things can be that are made to hold the same sort of little trinkets of love and memory that everybody else foregoes and forgets.

The ticket lay there a month and I never said a word, but I began to get my money back right away. I tripped up the rounds of the golden ladder every day, and, strange to tell, I was totally unable to *stop* going up until I reached the top and stood with both feet perched upon " $100,000 in gold." I tried to steady myself a little and be persuaded that $25,000 would be comfortable. I did my best to cultivate a sentiment of respect for $50,000, but the paltry sum sank below the horizon, and like the Spaniard overwhelmed at sight of the sea, who went down upon his knees on Gilboa or somewhere, I saw nothing but the golden ocean of $100,000. And why not? Was not the one quite as easy to get as the other? To be sure, in the glow of my story the capital prize that stood upon its head as a pyramid, has been fashioned into a ladder like Jacob's, with the angels of Imagination and Fancy going up and down thereon, and at last all melted into a sea, has inundated the whole landscape; but I tell you a man with a hundred thousand dollars may defy rhetoric and mixed metaphors with impunity.

I thought I would make my will, and " give and bequeath to my well-beloved wife Lucy" fifty thousand dollars. When I had counted this out by itself, the heap of gold glittered so that it dazzled me out of my discretion, and I asked

Lucy, in a quiet way, whether if I had $100,000
in gold and should will her fifty thousand free
and clear, it would be enough. She laughed and
said she thought it would be liberal! I then
told her what I had done. Now, Lucy is pretty
square-cornered mentally, but she comes of a
stock on the mother's side somewhat given to
dreaming. That mother of hers—she is seventy-
six if she is a day—will see as much beauty in
the sky and breathe the fragrance of the apple-
blossoms with as fresh a pleasure as if the world
were only sixteen years old, and world and woman
were born twins. She will sit down any time
upon a damp bank of crimson and gold cloud
that flanks the sunset, and never think of taking
cold more than she did forty years ago. She is
always seeing faces in the fire, and laying plans
that will never be hatched, and altogether has a
thousand luxuries that the tax-gatherer can not
possibly get into his schedule. Lucy betrays her
lineage. When I give her a "ten" sometimes,
she will fold her arms, swing slowly to and fro
in the rocking-chair, and pay it all out over and
over, and get her money's worth in ever so many
things useful and beautiful, and the green-backed
decimal will be snugly lying all the while in
that same box of momentous trifles. I think ten
dollars go as far with Lucy as twenty-five do

with most people, and by the same sign make her two and a half times as happy.

" Port "—that is the name of my boy—saw not a glimmer of gold for days and days after Lucy had her saffronian vision. He toiled on like Bunyan's fellow with the muck-rake at his calling, nor saw the angel, golden even as a sunflower, that floated overhead. It seemed a pity to wrong him out of his inheritance, and so I told him. I said, " Port, we are a rich family," and showed him the strip of paper. He ticked off the figures slowly, like a clock just running down, 1-0-4-1-6-3, and said—nothing. I thought he lacked gratitude, and so I made a plunge into the dark ages for something to punish him with, and came up with the brand-new fact that ingratitude is a crime so base the ancients never thought it worth while to make a law against it, as nobody, probably, would ever be guilty of it. " Port " went out, and I at once set about erasing the last cypher of the bequest I had made the boy, so that what had read $10,000 became $1,000, and I devised all the rest for the cultivation of gratitude in the human family.

Meanwhile the days grew shorter and shorter, like the strings of David's harp, and October was about done, and the drawing was at hand. But what mattered it all? We had entered into

possession already. We had invested one hundred
thousand of the prize in the best of securities,
and we were receiving eight thousand dollars a
year, for you see it was $100,000 in gold, to-
wit: $113,000 in greenbacks. We owed no man
anything. We had traveled all over the broad
domain of Columbus' magnificent " find." We
had given two thousand dollars a year to objects
of benevolence. We had bought exquisite works
of art, and sent a dozen poor painters of good
pictures abroad. We had imported rare old English books and strewn them upon our tables and
given them to our neighbors. We presented an
illustrated copy of " Paradise Lost " to our wood-
sawyer one day, a copy reinforced like his
breeches, with leather, and he was very grateful,
and sat down upon it when he ate his bread
and cheese and said it was " good," and we
were gratified. We purchased a sober horse and
a modest carriage, and propped up the line fence
and shingled the kitchen. In a word, the gaunt
wolf I had been trying for years to keep away
from the door, had been brained at last with a
golden club, and his skin lay upon the carriage
floor for a foot-robe.

There was a legion of people we wanted to
help — a great many of them when we first began, and I told Lucy to get a quire of paper
and make a catalogue, but somehow or other they

got fewer as we thought about it, until she numbered every one upon her fingers that seemed to
have much hold upon our affections. Those I
pensioned off in the most liberal manner, and
had quite a warm and genial feeling about my
heart, as if I had really been beneficent and *done*
something, when I had only been benevolent and
wished something. We had two or three wealthy
neighbors who had gathered richness as damp
logs gather moss, and that was about all there
was of it — aggregating golden egg after golden
egg, flattening themselves out like an incubating
goose ambitious to cover the whole nest, and
calling the proceeding "enterprise." I would set
these mossy fellows an example that should re-
buke them to the tips of their ears. And so I
gave twenty thousand dollars for a public library
to be free to all residents of the town forever.
We had made Christmas "merry" and New Year
"happy" for many a heart that would else have
had neither one nor the other.

I am glad now to be able to state that there
was only one man whom I had the least desire
to humble when I became an hundred thousand
strong, and he was an insurance agent — a retired
doctor, who, growing weary of saving lives with
pills, had taken to insuring lives with policies.
He was always tormenting me "to insure." He
looked me over like an undertaker with a mea-

sure in his eye. He kept me constantly reminded
of the fact of death, as if it were inevitable. I
hardly ever saw him that I did not fancy him
rushing around to my widow the next day after
I had won the wager, paying her the amount of
insurance, and thence away to the printing office
with a card flickering in his hand, inscribed with
words and figures following, to-wit:

AGENT OF THE SO-AND-SO INSURANCE CO.:

   I thank you for the prompt payment of the sum of $10,000,
for which amount you had insured my late husband's life.

                       Gratefully,   LUCY.

Late husband indeed! The pulses of a pound
of cold putty are lively compared with my circulation at the idea of that sort of " late " —
too late ever to be again " on time." Well, all
I want of that doctor is that he shall solicit me
once more, when I will say, " Insure? Do I
look like a man who needs help for his perish-
ing family? Examine my will — Lucy, $50,000!
' Port,' $20,000 ! Accept an invitation to my
Free Library. Be silent and be happy. Good
morning," and with this nightcap for his impor-
tunity, I would pass graciously on like a great
harvest-moon when it gives the last touch to the
ripening regiments of corn.

   And the thirty-first of October came at last,
and the supreme hour for the turn of the wheel

away there in the city of the Golden Gate, but what should I care? The capital prize had all been won, and invested, and given away and expended. I had *rehearsed* the fortune and it had left no corroding care — that word "corroding," heart-gnawing it *ought* to mean; think of a lively rodent, say a squirrel, in a beating heart! — had kindled no passion, scattered no Greek fire of pride or envy anywhere. What *more* need I desire, and yet I could hardly help wondering if they knew I had purchased the ticket 104,163; whether when — not if, for there is never an "if" in the land of dreams and of Spain — when the capital prize should be declared off to me out of the great wheel, they would not telegraph me at once from San Francisco, for I certainly would pay the expense without a murmur. I went to the door once or twice to see if the telegraph messenger might not be coming, and I at once gave him one hundred dollars in gold. But night distanced the telegram and reached me first. Possibly, though, the agent in Chicago may write me by the evening mail, and I gave one hundred dollars in gold to the man that licked the envelope, and one hundred dollars in gold to the man who delivered the letter. But the mail came and the letter did not. I was sorry for the loss the clerk in the post-office had suffered, and made up my mind to make him librarian of my

26

Free Library at a salary of a thousand dollars a year.

Along in the evening Lucy and I had a little discussion as to whether we should not take the prize in gold, say double eagles, and put them all to roost on the dining table, and call in a few friends to see the golden aviary with its blessed birds of Paradise, and borrow the neighbor's steelyards, as somebody did in the touching story of the " Forty Thieves," or some other Arabian Night's entertainment, and weigh the hundred thousand avoirdupois, and then send it back to Chicago and have the dead metal return all in full leaf, green as Valambrosa, say an hundred 1,000-dollar bills, or a thousand 100-dollar bills, Lucy and I could hardly tell which.

The first of November dawned as brightly as November ever dawns, and with it came the tidings that my " $100,000 in gold " had somehow, by mistake no doubt, been drawn by somebody else, and that ticket 104,163 was worth — well — about a twist for a cigar - lighter ! My imagination slipped down the golden ladder that, like the Patriarch's, had an angel at the top and a pillow of stone at the bottom — slipped down from its high estate and made a Rachel of itself, " and would not be comforted." I left the parlor, where I had been sitting for the last month because I thought I could afford to, and went away disconsolate into the kitchen, but "Willie," the mocking bird, was singing a pleasant song. I returned to the parlor and Lucy, the heiress to the half of my fortune, was laughing a pleasant laugh, and "Port," whom I had forgiven in a codicil, and left $20,000, said he did not care a "Continental" for the whole business, which, considering that Continental currency, toward the last of it, was sold low, at about so much a peck, "dry measure," may be taken as a pretty forcible expression of his perfect cheerfulness under the disaster.

But *was* it a disaster? Had I not had the prize, and enjoyed it and shared it and bequeathed it? My fortune had never tempted a thief. It had neither put the prayer of the Lord nor of Agur out of fashion: "Give us this day our daily bread!" "Give me neither poverty nor riches!" So far as I have heard, "104,163" was the lucky number after all, and I certainly believe nobody ever before received so much for so little — $100,000 in imperishable gold for five dollars and sixty-five cents, true coin of the realm of an imagination and a fancy both warmed into a life curiously fresh and new by the touch of a hope, never to be realized, of mere material wealth.

"One blast upon a bugle horn,"—if we may trust a man who was more conscientious in the

telling of fiction than most men are in relating
the truth,— was " worth a thousand men." Jericho came down at the blast of a horn.

Fame's shall give breath, and all the land
shall give heed. Gabriel's shall sound, and the
dead shall be intent. But cornucopia the golden
is the *exalted* horn among the nations. They
always see the glittering millions lavished from
the broader end that flares and blossoms- like a
tulip, but it is strange they do not oftener dis-
cern the diminished man coming out at the other
and the lesser end of the self-same horn. The
wealth may make a ladder and rig it out with
rounds commanding loftier planes and broader
views, but there must be a foot bold enough to
climb them, and a brain balanced enough to regard the grander horizons and the growing lights
undizzied and undazzled, and a heart true enough
to be touched and softened and kindled by it
all into the living belief that these words are
worthy of all acceptation : " Faith, Hope, Charity
—these three, but the GREATEST of these is
Charity." A belief lodged in the head is *there*,
but a belief lodged in the heart is *every*where.

As for Lucy and I, our " castles in Spain " are
all builded and peopled, the lawns around them
are Elysian, the sky above them is clear heaven,
sunshine plays forever around their purple towers.
Let us make fast the door against the wolf we

thought we had killed with a bludgeon of gold, and betake ourselves again with cheerfulness and content to our possessions in Spain — ours forever and a day by the power of the charm that lay hid in the ticket I purchased — and Lucy, "Port" and I do earnestly wish that all the readers of this chapter from life, if they do not draw the Capital Prize, may at least gain that next best thing — the treasure wrapped up, like a rose in a bud, in Number 104,163.

CHAPTER III.

OUR OLD GRANDMOTHER.

"I FIND the marks of my shortest steps beside those of my beloved mother, which were measured by my own," says Dumas, and so conjures up one of the sweetest images in the world. He was revisiting the home of his infancy; he was retracing the little paths around it in which he had once walked; and strange flowers could not efface, and rank grass could not conceal, and cruel ploughs could not obliterate, his "shortest footsteps," and his mother's beside them, measured by his own.

And who needs to be told whose footsteps they were that thus kept time with the feeble pattering of childhood's little feet? It was no mother beside whom Ascanius walked " with equal steps " in Virgil's line, but a strong, stern man, who could have borne him and not been burdened; folded him in his arms from all danger and not been wearied; everything, indeed, he could have done for him, but just what he needed most — could not sympathize with him — he could not be a child again. Ah, a rare art is that, — for, indeed, it is an art, to set back the great old clock of time and be a boy once more! Man's imagination can easily see the child a man; but how hard it is for it to see the man a child; and he who had learned to glide back into that rosy time when he did not know that thorns were under the roses, or that clouds would ever return after the rain; when he thought a tear could stain a cheek no more than a drop of rain a flower; when he fancied that life had no disguise, and hope no blight at all — has come as near as anybody can to discovering the North-west passage to Paradise.

And it is, perhaps, for this reason that it is so much easier for a mother to enter the kingdom of Heaven than it is for the rest of the world. She fancies she is leading the children, when, after all, the children are leading her, and they keep her, indeed, where the river is narrowest, and the air is clearest; and the beckoning of the radiant band is so plainly seen from the other side, that it is no wonder she so often lets go her clasp upon the little finger she is holding, and goes over to the neighbor's, and the children follow like lambs to the fold; for we think it ought somewhere to be written: "Where the mother is, there will the children be also."

But it was not of the mother, but of the dear old-fashioned grandmother, whose thread of love spun "by hand" on life's little wheel, and longer and stronger than they make it now, was wound around and about the children she saw playing in the children's arms, in a true love-knot that nothing but the shears of Atropos could sever; for do we not recognize the lambs sometimes, when summer days are over and autumn winds are blowing, as they come bleating from the yellow fields, by the crimson thread we wound about their necks in April or May, and so undo the gate and let the wanderers in?

Blessed be the children who have an old-fashioned grandmother. As they hope for length of days let them love and honor her, for we can tell them they will never find another.

There is a large old kitchen somewhere in the past, and an old-fashioned fireplace therein, with its smooth old jambs of stone — smooth with many knives that have been sharpened there — smooth with many little fingers that have clung there. There are andirons, too — the old andirons, with rings in the top, whereon many temples of flame have been builded, with spires and turrets of crimson. There is a broad, worn hearth, worn by feet that have been torn and bleeding by the way, or been made "beautiful," and walked upon floors of tesselated gold. There are tongs

in the corner, wherewith we grasped a coal, and
" blowing for a little life," lighted our first candle ; there is a shovel, wherewith were drawn
forth the glowing embers in which we saw our
first fancies and dreamed our first dreams — the
shovel with which we stirred the sleepy logs till
the sparks rushed up the chimney as if a forge
were in blast below, and wished we had so many
lambs, so many marbles, or so many somethings
that we coveted ; and so it was we wished our
first wishes.

There is a chair — a low, rush-bottom chair ;
there is a little wheel in the corner, a big wheel
in the garret, a loom in the chamber. There
are chests full of linen and yarn, and quilts of
rare pattern, and samples in frames.

And everywhere and always the dear old wrink-
led face of her whose firm, elastic step mocks
the feeble saunter of her children's children —
the old-fashioned grandmother of twenty years
ago. She, the very Providence of the old homestead — she who loved us all, and said she wished
there were more of us to love, and took all the
school in the Hollow for grand-children besides.
A very expansive heart was hers, beneath that
woolen gown, or that more stately bombazine, or
that sole heir-loom of silken texture.

We can see her to-day, those mild blue eyes,
with more of beauty in them than time could

27*

touch or death do more than hide — those eyes
that held both smiles and tears within the faint-
est call of every one of us, and soft reproof, that
seemed not passion but regret.   A white tress
has escaped from beneath her snowy cap; she
has just restored a wandering lamb to its mother;
she lengthened the tether of a vine that was
straying over a window, as she came in, and
plucked a four-leaved clover for Ellen.   She sits
down by the little wheel — a tress is running
through her fingers from the distaff's disheveled
head, when a small voice cries "Grandma!"
from the old red cradle, and "Grandma!"
Tommy shouts from the top of the stairs.   Gently
she lets go the thread, for her patience is almost
as beautiful as her charity, and she touches the
little bark in a moment, till the young voyager
is in a dream again, and then directs Tommy's
unavailing attempts to harness the cat.   The tick
of the clock runs faint and low, and she opens
the mysterious door and proceeds to wind it up.
We are all on tip-toe, and we beg in a breath
to be lifted up one by one, and look in the
hundredth time upon the tin cases of the weights,
and the poor lonely pendulum, which goes to
and fro by its little dim window, and never
comes out in the world, and our petitions are
all granted, and we are lifted up, and we all

touch with a finger the wonderful weights, and the music of the little wheel is resumed.

Was Mary to be married, or Jane to be wrapped in a shroud? So meekly did she fold the white hands of the one upon her still bosom, that there seemed to be a prayer in them there; and so sweetly did she wreathe the white rose in the hair of the other, that one would not have wondered had more roses budded for company.

How she stood between us and apprehended harm; how the rudest of us softened beneath the gentle pressure of her faded and tremulous hand! From her capacious pocket that hand was ever withdrawn closed, only to be opened in our own, with the nuts she had gathered, the cherries she had plucked, the little egg she had found, the "turn-over" she had baked, the trinket she had purchased for us as the product of her spinning, the blessing she had stored for us — the offspring of her heart.

What treasures of story fell from those old lips; of good fairies and evil, of the old times when she was a girl; and we wondered if ever — but then she could n't be handsomer or dearer — but that she ever was "little." And then, when we begged her to sing! "Sing us one of the old songs you used to sing mother, grandma."

" Children, I can't sing," she always said; and

mother used to lay her knitting softly down, and
the kitten stopped playing with the yarn upon
the floor, and the clock ticked lower in the corner, and the fire died down to a glow, like an
old heart that is neither chilled nor dead, and
grandmother sang.   To be sure it would n't do
for the parlor and the concert-room now-a-days;
but then it was the old kitchen and the old-
fashioned grandmother, and the old ballad, in the
dear old times, and we can hardly see to write
for the memory of them, though it is a hand's
breadth to the sunset.

Well, she sang.   Her voice was feeble and
wavering, like a fountain just ready to fail, but
then how sweet-toned it was; and it became
deeper and stronger, but it could n't grow sweeter.   What "joy of grief" it was to sit there
around the fire, all of us, except Jane, that
clasped a prayer to her bosom, and her we thought
we saw, when the hall-door was opened a moment by the wind; but then we were not afraid,
for was n't it her old smile she wore? — to sit
there around the fire, and weep over the woes
of the "Babes in the Wood," who lay down
side by side in the great solemn shadows; and
how strangely glad we felt when the robin-red-
breast covered them with leaves, and last of all
when the angels took them out of the night
into Day Everlasting.

We may think what we will of it now, but
the song and the story heard around the kitchen
fire have colored the thoughts and lives of most
of us; have given us the germs of whatever
poetry blesses our hearts; whatever memory blooms
in our yesterdays. Attribute whatever we may
to the school and the school-master, the rays
which make that little day we call life, radiate
from the God-swept circle of the hearthstone.

Then she sings an old lullaby she sang to
mother—*her* mother sang to her; but she does
not sing it through, and falters ere 't is done.
She rests her head upon her hands, and it is
silent in the old kitchen. Something glitters
down between her fingers and the firelight, and
it looks like rain in the soft sunshine. The old
grandmother is thinking when she first heard the
song, and of the voice that sang it, when a
light-haired and light-hearted girl she hung around
that mother's chair, nor saw the shadows of the
years to come. O! the days that are no more!
What spell can we weave to bring them back
again? What words can we unsay, what deeds
undo, to set back, just this once, the ancient
clock of time?

So all our little hands were forever clinging
to her garments, and staying her as if from
dying, for long ago she had done living for herself, and lived alone in us. But the old kitchen

wants a presence to-day, and the rush-bottomed chair is tenantless.

How she used to welcome us when we were grown, and came back once more to the homestead.

We thought we were men and women, but we were children there. The old-fashioned grandmother was blind in the eyes, but she saw with her heart, as she always did. We threw our long shadows through the open door, and she felt them as they fell over her form, and she looked dimly up and saw tall shapes in the door-way, and she says, "Edward I know, and Lucy's voice I can hear, but whose is that other? It must be Jane's," for she had almost forgotten the folded hands. "Oh, no, not Jane, for she — let me see — she is waiting for me, isn't she?" and the old grandmother wandered and wept.

"It is another daughter, grandmother, that Edward has brought," says some one, "for your blessing."

"Has she blue eyes, my son? Put her hand in mine, for she is my latest born, the child of my old age. Shall I sing you a song, children?" Her hand is in her pocket as of old; she is idly fumbling for a toy, a welcome gift to the children that have come again.

"Come, children, sit around the fire. Shall I sing you a song, or tell you a story? Stir the fire, for it is cold ; the nights are growing colder."

The clock in the corner struck nine, the bed-time of those old days. The song of life was indeed sung, the story told, it was bed-time at last. Good night to thee, grandmother! The old-fashioned grandmother was no more, and we miss her forever. But we will set up a tablet in the midst of the memory, in the midst of the heart, and write on it only this:

SACRED TO THE MEMORY

OF THE

OLD-FASHIONED GRANDMOTHER.

GOD BLESS HER FOR EVER.

CHAPTER IV.

OUT-DOOR PREACHING.

THE miracle of Spring is beginning.

Leafless, indeed, stand the great woods, and shivering in the cold North wind. The joints of rheumatic oaks creak dismally, and there is a moan in the maples. The skeleton orchards are gray and brown upon the Southern slopes, but the sun is shining and the clock of Time ticks in the heart of May. A January fire rolls and roars up the chimney's capacious throat; the water-pail is nightly glazed with ice, but the birds are abroad and their songs are in all the air. Not a wisp of hay remains in the wide, deep bay of the barn, and the cows decline " to give down," and the lambs are going where the good lambs go, though the lilacs are budding and the willows have fringed the streams with green.

How full of the dear old music of Summer are wood, orchard and field. Even the great empty barn, with its ribs of oak, is a-twitter with swallows that dart in and out at the diamond doors in the gables, and the mud-walled cottages that are built along the rafters. The robins are singing the self-same song they sang a thousand years ago, and the finches are untarnished and golden as ever. Down by the marsh the bobo'-links are ringing their little bells, and swinging to and fro upon the little bushes that sway in the wind. The brown thrushes have built their nests in the fence-corners and the heaps of brush; a Baltimore oriole flickered like a flake of fire through the garden, this morning, and drifted away behind the barn; we frightened up a whip-poor-will yesterday, from among the withered leaves, and found a blue-bird's nest with a single egg in a hollow stump in the pasture. A little gray couple are busy building in the cleft of the bar-post, and a small Trojan in speckled jacket is about to keep house on the loaded end of the well-sweep that goes up forty times a day and comes down with a bang. Why did n't the little idiot take up his quarters in the bucket! A fortnight ago, John hung his jacket upon the fence, and to-day he shook out from one of the pockets a nest, and two eggs as blue as the sky.

There is singing everywhere: from the tuft of gray grass there comes a small tune of two notes and a rest, then two more; from the second rail of the fence a gush of melody; from the roof-ridge, a solo; from the depths of the air, as of angel calling unto angel. The birds and the buds make it May, and May it shall be.

Yesterday was Sunday, as clear and as cool as charity, and yesterday I got into good company for once in a way, and went to church in the woods. The gray temple that God built looked dull and empty as I approached, but as I entered, the birds were singing an anthem and Nature had begun to work a miracle.

Last winter we floundered to the January service, and the drifts, how huge they were, and the white arms of the forest were stretched out in silent benediction, stern and cold, like the blessing of old Puritans.

Now, the earth is strewn with withered leaves of a gone summer that rustled articulately beneath the thoughtful foot, and said, as words can never say it: "In the midst of life we are in death," and thus the Sermon began.

And then the birds all around joined in to sing, and the wood-dove to mourn with her mate, and so this passage of Scripture was read out: "The winter is over and gone; the time of the singing of birds is come, and the voice of the turtle is heard in the land."

And after that, two sparrows who were blown away last autumn by the keen Northeaster, and that nobody thought to see again, sang a simple song, the burden whereof was, "Not a sparrow falleth to the ground without Him."

A delicate white flower, that had lifted away a counterpane of damp gray leaves, stood up in its place at the foot of a great tree, and what did we have then, but "Thou fool, that which thou sowest is not quickened except it die. Behold, I show you a mystery! we shall not all sleep, but we shall all be changed."

And the little stars of pink and white flowers that were clustered in a constellation about the mossy rock, lifted up their voices and sang, even as they did in Time's morning: "There is one glory of the sun, and another glory of the moon, and another glory of the stars; for one star differeth from another star in glory. So also is the resurrection of the dead." And thus the doctrine was demonstrated, and a robin that minute began to sing.

Then there went noiselessly over the dead leaves as they lay, and over the preachers, and over them that prayed, a small shadow; and, looking up, a white breath of cloud was drifting by, and it said as it went, "Thus passeth human life," and the wind breathed a low sigh, and the service went on.

And all the while the birds were busy as busy could be, carrying timbers and tapestry and couches

of down for the homes they were building, and
one sang as she wrought, " The better the day,"
and her mate took it up with " The better the
deed," and the Sabbath unbroken shone on.

A few bees, brave as their fellows that dared
the dead lion of old Samson's time, went trum-
peting along the neighboring fields, a feeble
charge against the living lion of the North.
Walking along the grand old aisles upon whose
floor last summer's dead were lying, let us recall
the time before the first snow fell, and the re-
lenting year looked back and smiled, so sad and
sweet a smile, even as our dead who stand sometimes upon the holy threshold of a dream;
when the last breath of those dead leaves went
heavenward like a prayer, and Indian Summer
charmed the drowsy earth and golden air.
But there is no dying now. The graves are
opened! Lo, the violet comes; the lady-slippers
dance upon the air while wild Sweet Williams
stand admiring by.

Grand sermons preached they all, of faith and
hope and beauty yet to be, and as you turned
away, there in the field a passage from the Sermon on the Mount, wrapped in green silk, was
lying, and what was it but, "Behold the lilies
of the field, how they grow, they toil not, neither
do they spin, and yet Solomon in all his glory
was not arrayed like one of these."

So with fragments of sermons and snatches of songs strewn along the way, you leave the temple of the Lord and bear away with you some of the preachers and some of the singers and some of the beauties of the great congregation in that mighty minster. You dismantle a fallen tree of one of Nature's studies, a broad green mat of moss, a piece of velvet from the very loom that wove the glory of morning, and bear it home for Sunday Reading. Perusing it awhile, you wonder you could ever have set foot on such a dainty piece of work, for there, written in God's "fine hand," are maple groves and close-fed pastures for some tiny herd; and little pines like filaments of feathers; and emerald hills full-crowned with woods; and in small valleys, like dimples in a baby's cheek, a mimic lily, as starlight in a tear; the least of Alps with sand-grain cliffs; spears for atomies, tipped with a drop of red; trees a full round inch in height, touched at the top with something like a sunset; a clover-field broad as a linnet's wing, and tufts of shrubs that might hide a hunted gnat from some small sportsman in those mimic fields; a landscape done in little; a picture Nature painted on Holidays and Sundays, and so hid death that, in some fallen tree, lay like a Titan all abroad.

And this bright landscape fair as Eden land, unrolled upon a dinner plate, was served up for

Love-of-Beauty's feast, where Fancy sat as guest, and Hope stood by. How earnest Nature is in all she does; how finished, all her work from moss to mountain. The tint on girlhood's lip is well laid on, indeed, but with no greater care than set these rubies in the green fields of Moss-land.

And so that plate of moss "reads like a book." A month ago those pines were not; nay, the small mountain where they grow was not embossed upon the velvet, and here you look upon the *programme* of what Earth shall be — the finished miracle of Spring; what Earth shall be, despite complaint and evil prophecy.

Take Nature at her word, even as the birds that trust her, and so toil and sing though snows have drifted to the heart of May. Look not abroad for token that the end is near. No telescope shall ever bring to view time's brown October. But when the birds forget to build their summer homes and bless the woods, and roses lose their flush and fragrance; when on just such another scroll of mossy landscape as you are reading now, no promises are made, then know that earnest Nature has wearied of her work and seeks a Holiday at last.

CHAPTER V.

THE STORY OF THE BELL.

THE Roman knight who rode, all accoutred as he was, into the gulf, and the mouth of the hungry Forum closed upon him and was satisfied, vanquished, in his own dying, that great Philistine, Oblivion, which, sooner or later, will conquer us all.

But there is an old story that always charmed me more. In some strange land and time they were about to cast a bell for a mighty tower; a hollow, starless heaven of iron. It should toll for dead monarchs —" the king is dead!"—and make glad clamor for the new prince —" long live the king!" It should proclaim so great a passion or so grand a pride that either would be worship, or, wanting these, forever hold its peace.

Now this bell was not to be digged out of the cold mountains; it was to be made of something that had been warmed with a human touch or loved with a human love. And so the people came like pilgrims to a shrine, and cast their offerings into the furnace and went away. There were links of chains that bondmen had worn bright, and fragments of swords that had broken in heroes' hands. There were crosses and rings and bracelets of fine gold; trinkets of silver and toys of poor red copper. They even brought things that were licked up in an instant by the red tongues of flame; good words they had written and flowers they had cherished; perishable things that could never be heard in the rich tone and volume of the bell.

And the fires panted like a strong man when he runs a race, and the mingled gifts flowed down together and were lost in the sand, and the dome of iron was drawn out like leviathan.

And by-and-by the bell was alone in its chamber, and its four windows looked forth to the four quarters of heaven. For many a day it hung dumb; the winds came and went, but they only set it a sighing; birds came and went, and sang under its eaves, but it was an iron horizon of dead melody still. All the meaner strifes and passions of men rippled on below it. They out-groped the ants, and out-wrought the bees, and out-watched the Chaldean shepherds, but the chamber of the bell was as dumb as the pyramids.

At last there came a time when men grew

grand for right and truth, and stood shoulder to shoulder over all the land, and went down like reapers to the harvest of death; looked into the graves of them that slept, and believed there was something grander than living; glanced on into the far future and discerned there was something bitterer than dying, and so, standing between the quick and the dead, they quitted themselves like men.

Then the bell woke in its chamber, and the great waves of its music rolled gloriously out and broke along the blue walls of the world like an anthem; and every tone in it was familiar as a household word to somebody, and he heard it and knew it with a solemn joy. Poured into that fiery furnace-heart together, the humblest gifts were blent in one great wealth, and accents feeble as a sparrow's song grew eloquent and strong; and lo, a people's stately soul heaved on the tenth wave of a mighty voice!

We thank GOD in this our day for the furnace and the fire; for the offerings of gold and the trinkets of silver; for the good deed and the true word; for the great triumph and the little song.

29

CHAPTER VI.

"MY EYE!"

THAT sounds like slang, and I have quoted it
lest somebody should think it original; but then
there is really no more slang in it, as I apply
it, than there is in Agur's prayer — the man
who wanted what could be spared precisely as
well as not, and who proposed to make his pantaloons without any pockets. The application
changes the nature. Thus, I spread mustard
upon a piece of linen and clap it upon the nape
of a fellow's neck, and it is a blister. I veneer
therewith a pink and white slice of Israelitish
abomination, and protect it with a thin section
of bread, and it is — oh, blessed transformation!
— it is a sandwich! So with the topmost phrase
of this chapter; a boy without any brim to his
hat shouts it in the street, and it is slang;
but I take it to christen an essay as full of eyes
as Juno's Argus, and — *presto!* — it becomes a
Christian name.

Perhaps there is nothing of which there is so

many — if we except blades of grass and grains of sand — as eyes. From the potato that watches you *perdu* from its native hill, to a peacock's tail, about everything is gifted with an eye. There's the eye you put the thread through, and the eye which you catch with a hook, my girl, when you used to fasten your dress behind; and the eye of Day, and the Daisy, my poet; and the "dry eye," which we have been told once or twice that congregations were entirely out of. There's a violet in the garden-border with an eye of blue. There's a fly on the window-pane — six legs, and "eyes" enough in its head to carry any question with an overwhelming affirmative. There's "Black-eyed Susan," in the play, that makes you hum "All in the Downs the fleet was moored," and snuff salt water, and make a fool of yourself. I can recall but three things at the moment so poor as not to be blessed with at least two eyes: the needle, the Cyclops, and the man of one idea!

Homer — one of him — says Juno was ox-eyed; and though, from all accounts, Juno was rather a coarse creature, yet everybody has taken to likening his love to somebody's "nigh" ox; and there is something beautiful in the great lamp-like eyes of an amiable creature that comes meekly under the yoke and never makes complaint. Like Darwin's *other* monkeys, we are all imitative animals; and how many of us would ever have thought to look into a bullock's eyes at all if the blind native of seven cities had not set the example, nobody can tell; but then it is the Greek fashion to praise the women and the oxen in the same breath.

"Ladies and gentlemen, here is one of the most *veracious* animals that swims in the sea. He follers ships if so be somebody may be throwed overboard!"

The speaker was a rough man, with one arm and a grizzled lip. The subject of his discourse lay in a tank of water, and watched him as he talked. The thing was a sea-tiger, and resembled an exaggerated seal. Its large, round, dark head was lifted out of the water; but that head was illuminated by a pair of the most splendid eyes in the world. I can not say there was any trace of *soul* in them, albeit there might be a tender memory of the soles of the copper-toed shoes of the last little boy he had masticated and swallowed; but ah, those eyes!—they were large and gentle and pensive. You would n't have been a bit surprised had he burst out with one of Moore's melodies about

"No pearl ever lay under Oman's green water."

If the keeper was as "veracious" as he declared the tiger was, of a truth those eyes were the

most mendacious couple that ever kept company.
If there is no surviving relative to object, I
should like to call one of them Ananias and the
other Sapphira. It was a case of love at first
sight. Such wistful, melting glances as that
miserable beast turned upon the ladies who
shook their fans at him, and the little children
who "made eyes" at him in return, nobody but
a captivating woman could hope to rival.

The dingy plaster wall of a smoke-house is
as utterly blank as your last lottery ticket. Now
fancy the dirty leather apron of some son of
Vulcan hung ignobly thereon, and then fancy,
as you look at it, an impossible eye breaking out
all at once in an improbable place in that wall
and close to the apron—an eye small, twinkling,
uncertain, and you have the expression of an
elephant's countenance. And yet we boys and
girls have all been led up to Columbus, Hanni-
bal, Romeo, and the rest of them, and bidden
to mark the sagacious glitter of that sinister
crevice. The word "sagacity" is completely
ruined for all human uses. It belongs to the
baggage-smashers of the brute creation; and whenever you read of some "sagacious" statesman you
immediately think of an elephant. Without the
intelligence of a horse or the affection of a dog,
and with no beauty either of mould or motion,
the beast's eye tells the story of what Cooper's
Sachem calls "the hog with two tails."

The remembrance of an eye is the most tena-
cious of memories. You may forget the fashion
of face and figure, but if

> " There 's a light in the window for thee,"

the expression of an eye will sometimes be all
that remains to you of a dead friend. There it
is that the soul comes the nearest to escaping.
There it is more nearly undressed and out of
doors than it can possibly be any where else
without dying.

"Was Aaron Burr tall?" asked one woman
of another who once saw that recreant "child
of many prayers" just for one moment at Al-
bany.

"I do n't know," was the reply; "but such
a glance as he gave you! I have always remembered him as the man with the living eyes."
Ah, the flash of the soul's artillery has photo-
graphic powers beyond the art of the artist, and
its proofs, of all the printing in the world are
imperishable!

Do you remember the pretty pebbles you used
to gather out of the beds of the brooks — the
notes of the sweet low tune they ran by?
Dripping from the water, they were red rubies
and green garnets and golden opals and blue
sapphires — precious stones every one; but the
glory and glamour of the brooks once gone, they

grew dim and dull and valueless. It is so with human eyes. You can not always be sure of their color. A pale, light eye may deepen and darken, when the soul is stirred behind it, till you declare it black as midnight; and a brown eye may be fairly bleached blue in the light and fire of passion. The elder Booth's eyes were all colors in a night; and Charlotte Cushman's, as Meg Merrilies, kindled into a broad white blaze, like a pine-knot fire. A nose brought to an edge, and a couple of small black eyes, form, as astrologers say, " an inauspicious conjunction." Such eyes are apt to *snap*, a dreadful hemlock quality, to which a strabismus, so violent that the vicious members seem trying to get at each other under the bridge of the nose, is a blessing and a beauty. Let us not be censorious. Let us wish the owners of all such eyes a great deal of self-control, or a little of the grace of God.

But whatever you do, I pray you never call anybody's eyes " orbs," unless you are re-writing Milton's Paradise Lost. And do n't call them " organs." There was a country printer and editor whose wristbands would have been always in mourning with his hands, if he had worn a shirt, and who always had a stale copy of his paper sticking out of a side-pocket, and smelling musty—for he used poor ink and poor ideas

to match — and he was forever talking of his
" organ," wherever he was, and quoting from
his " organ," until people laughed about it, and
said " there was a complete outfit for some itinerant Italian with musical proclivities. There
was an ' organ,' and there was a monkey, and
nothing lacking but the man to grind it, and a
piece of green baize!" If you wish to know
about a word, set the children to using it. Fancy
little Johnny's cry of " Oh, I 've got something
in my organs!" or a sound of lamentation in
Ramah — leastwise in the door-yard — with Jenny's
wail that her sun-bonnet keeps tumbling over her
orbs! When children and grown folks talk alike,
and the boy speaks as if he were crazy, you may
be sure the man talks as if he were a fool.

I had a friend. He was murdered in Illinois.
The man that killed him was never so true to
anybody as was this friend to me and mine.
He was buried without song or sermon. He has
gone to a good place, if he has gone *any*where.
I am not certain, but I *hope* so, for there was
too much genuine nobility about him to perish
utterly away — to be snuffed out like a candle,
as if he had never been. His name was — PEDRO.
His eyes, dark in the shadow, russet in the sun,
talked English all the while. Wronged by word
or blow, they pleaded for him with a touching
pathos. Caressed, they laughed and sparkled like

living fountains. Stretched upon the threshold
in the genial sun, a large human content worth
praying for shone in his eyes. There was a
great deal too much meaning in them for a
creature whose "spirit goeth downward," and
almost enough for a being with a soul to be
saved. What gave those eyes their eloquence?
Did the mere machinery of a dog's life light
them up so wonderfully, wistfully, sorrowfully?
There were love in them, and hope and abiding
trust and an honest heart. What lacked he to
entitle him to two names like a Christian, instead of one? He knew plenty of people with
whom he never could have exchanged qualities
without getting the worst of the bargain. But
he did better than to be a contemptible man,
for he was a noble dog. His eyes look inquiringly, wistfully, after me through the shadows
of the years that are past. They are the immortal part of him. They will last out a human
memory. Hereaway! PEDRO! Hereaway!

The kernel of the proverb, "Love me, love
my dog," is that you are getting pretty near a
man when you have made friends with his dog.
Now, I hate "black and tans," the tantivying
creatures, their mouths full of needles, a bark as
sharp as a razor, and the whole case of instruments on all sides of you at once; but I insist

that I love dogs. "Black and tans" are *not* dogs; they are cutlery.

And now, to come right home and make a personal matter of it, this gossip would never have seen the light had I not suffered the temporary loss of one eye, and that set me thinking. Our "body servants," the most of them, came into the world as Noah's caravan went into the ark — in *pairs*. Two hands, two feet, two ears, two eyes; and they are matched spans, every one. The truth is, I never thought much about having any eyes at all until one of them went under a cloud. None of us do. A man never feels his ears, no matter how long they are, while they *work* well, unless he lays hold of them with his hands. With some men, though, their ears are their "best hold." So with the eyes. When the sight is keen and clear, we just take in day and its glories, and the charm of color, and the witchery of shadow, we hardly know how. We *feel* them no more than we do the window-panes through which come the sunset and the starlight. But let something go wrong, and you are brought to a lively sense of possession in a twinkling. You begin to discover how rich you were without knowing it, and what an incalculable blessing you would lose if only one eye should be extinguished. I breathed air one night, a while ago, that eight hundred friendly people had just breathed for me; and I stood with my left shoulder to an open window with a chill breeze through it, and my left eye fell to weeping for the folly of the thing; and then impalpable crows began to build a nest of most palpable sticks, and fairly filled the unfortunate eyrie until it ceased to be a window, and became a — *rookery!* And the eye was closed until the unseemly birds could be persuaded to build elsewhere.

I think, if you touch a man's eye roughly, you come within one of touching his soul; and I came to think at times that the crows were foraging in my perceptive faculties for material wherewith to put my eye out.

The first thing done was to pickle the offending member in strong brine, as if it were an onion; but the miserable business of corvine nidification went on. Had you thrust both those hard words into my eye together, it could n't have hurt me a bit worse than the crows did.

Having made pickles, it was thought best to put up a sardine or two. Flax seed was expressed and impressed in an oleaginous bag, whose slippery contents wriggled about on the tremulous lid like a packet of angle-worms. But the crows liked linseed and kept on. Things looked serious, as far as I could see them with a solitary eye; but there was a comfort: if I had half as many eyes, I had twice as many

friends, and they were tender-hearted women. I
was a sort of Mungo Park, in a small way, only
I had a wife to look into my eye whenever I
asked her, which was every few minutes; and
I was n't in Africa, and I did n't lie under a
tree, and my female friends were not negroes,
and they did n't sing,

> " He has no mother to bring him milk,
> No wife to grind his corn."

With these exceptions I was *precisely* like
Mungo Park. The ladies were solicitous and
helpful. One suggested bread and milk; it was
brought and set upon the top of the stove.
Another, an alum curd; it was made and set
under the stove. A third, Thompson's Eye-water;
it was brought and thrown into the stove. A
fourth, Pettit's Eye-salve; it appeared and was
set upon the table.

Sandwiches were pronounced good; and hand-
breadths of mustard, tawnier than the river
Tiber, were spread behind my ears, and a care-
less crow dropped a stick or two. It was getting
too warm for them, but I could not see why.
In fact, I could n't see much of anything. It
grew warm; it waxed hot. The skin rolled up
like tattered bits of parchment, and the sandwich
lunch was over.

It was time to call the Doctor. He came.

Shrewd, skillful, patient, he mastered the situation. He saw the dishes of sea-water standing about, and the bags of linseed, and the plasters of mustard, and the alum curds, and the lotions, and the unguents, and he fell upon my eye, and he opened it as a Baltimore boy opens an oyster. He got no help from me; but he saw the crows. Looking about, he took a rapid inventory of what there was in the room that had not already been put into my eye. He gazed inquiringly at the bureau and a large rocking-chair. The sheet of zinc on which the stove stood arrested his attention. " You have n't used that, have you?" " No," said I; and he whipped out a little bottle, said " *Zinc*," shook it, pried open my eye with an earnestness that would not be denied, and poured the zinc square into it. Did you ever lie on your back in the bottom of a shot-tower when they were raining lead? If you never did, you do n't want to. And then the Doctor rolled my unfortunate optic about like a billiard ball, until the liquid was swashed over the whole surface. I thought then, and I still think, he meant to burn up the crows' nest, possibly the crows. That eye was better; the birds dropped a few more sticks; but they hung about the old place still.

It was then thought best to give the cellar the usual spring cleaning, and feed the pig with

the product. Rotten apples were recommended;
and a Russet, that needed to be sent to the
cooper's, leaned lazily over to one side on a
little plate, ready for use.

A kind lady from Massachusetts, for whose
interest I shall always be grateful, said that hen
and chickens were good — hen and chickens
smothered in cream. That puzzled me. It was
too late for hens and too early for chickens.
But the lady set a dozen pairs of little nimble
feet flying about the neighborhood for the poultry; and one day she came, bringing a handful
of small, green plants, chuckle-headed and cunning, and the secret of the fowls was out. They
were " house-leeks." The brood was put in a
tumbler and placed upon the bureau.

But the mischief went on in the aviary. I
think one of the crows was setting, ready to lay
or hatch, or something, while the other was
building a door-yard fence. It was the ninth
day, when even puppies pass the limit of total
eclipse, and something must be done. Another
lady, also from the Bay State, proposed, as the
cooking and baking had been done, and the pig
comforted, that we should feed the — *sheep!* She
named carrots. The girls down stairs were set
to washing carrots, and the procession of the
golden vegetable began to move. First, a boy
with a carrot in his claw, like Jupiter's eagle

with a thunderbolt in his talon. Then a lady
with a carrot on a tea-plate. Then a man with
an immense fellow on a platter. Then more carrots. Last, a grater, and the business began.
My patient, anxious wife sat up all night grat-
ing carrots. It sounded, in the middle watches,
like the rasp of a distant saw-mill. Everything
was the color of Ophir. For twenty-four hours,
once in eighteen minutes, did she apply that carrot; and the crows began to grow uneasy. Their
nest began to tumble to pieces. The repeated
and tremendous assaults proved too much for
them. The eye that had looked like an angry
moon in a watery sky began to clear up, and
recover its blue-white porcelain look once more.

The bandage was whipped off; but the team
did n't pull even. My right eye had gone ahead
in the business of seeing, and straightened the
traces till they twanged like fiddle-strings. The
left eye was drooping and languid. Things had
a cloudy look. I saw two doctors, when only
one had come in. I had two wives, with a face
apiece, growing on a single stem, like a couple
of cherries. My Massachusetts friends came in
with their doubles. But the worst of it was, I
had four feet, like a quadruped. Think of the
expense! Imagine the boots! It was a worry.
But I began this article. The crows are taking
flight — to return, I trust, in the only English
Poe's raven ever knew — "nevermore." .

I am indebted to the Doctor and I always mean to be. There can be no doubt that he made those crows uneasy. The zinc was worse than the crows, and they could not abide peacefully in one place. He has gone into the eye-business altogether, for he is a Surgeon in the Navy. He is going to *sea*.

The brightest May sun breaks out of the cloud. It kindles the hills; it touches up the woods, just ready to bud. A robin sings that same old song by the window.

Thank GOD for Light. His resplendent creation — Light, that came into being the moment He called it, like an instant and ready angel, watching at His feet.

Thank GOD for eyes — the most delicate and exquisite of all our servants. Let us be Persians, and worship the Sun. Let us be Israelites, and pray with our faces toward the EAST.

CHAPTER VII.

THE OLD ROAD.

In almost every old neighborhood there is an old road, disused and half forgotten, and we like to get away from the traveled thoroughfare, and wander, in a summer's day, along its deserted route.

Our grandfathers had a species of indomitable directness in making roads and making love that was wonderful to see. They did not believe in the line of beauty; there was nothing curvilinear about them, either in word or deed. They went by square and compass, and life and religion were laid out like Solomon's Temple. And so, straight over the hill, and right through the big timber, and plump into the swamp, and bounce over the "corduroy," went the old road.

Its long bridges are broken and mossy now, and brown birds in white waistcoats build nests beneath them, undisturbed by the small thunder of the rumbling wheels.

Nobody goes that way, not even the boys

bound out for school; for, ever so many years ago, in a November day, they have heard, a stranger went down by the old mill — you can see the rim of its dry gray wheel from here — and was never heard of more.

Years after, among the hemlocks, human bones were found, and to this day, on windy nights, groans come out of the gulf, and the troubled ghost is thought to be walking still.

Over yonder are a broad-disked sunflower and a heap of stone. The latter was once a hearth, for a house stood there, and after the stranger disappeared the tenant grew suddenly rich, as the times went, and showed gold with unknown words upon it, that none of the neighbors could make out, and pretty soon he took all that he had and went West; as some said to the " Genesee Country," and others to " the Ohio," which was yet more like a dream than the Genesee.

After that, nobody would live in the house, and it grew ruinous, and was haunted, and people saw a light there in dark nights, or thought they did, and the children shunned it, except in the brightest of mornings, when the sun was shining and the birds were singing, and the cows went lowing, Indian file, to the pasture; and after awhile, the old house tumbled down and crumbled away. Such stories thrive along old roads, even as the Mayweed, and the thistles, that nobody ever cuts, and on whose pink tops the yellow-birds rock up and down, like little boats at anchor, till the Fall winds whistle away the golden birds and the white down.

Even the brooks that used to tinkle across the track and under the little bridges, have somehow run dry, or gone another way, and you will see an old trough, dusty and bleached, by the road-side, the strip of bark, that brought the water from the hills, broken and scattered, and the earth worn hard and smooth with the tramping of many feet. Very long ago, a tin cup used to hang there, tethered with a string, for the sake of thirsty travelers. We like to stand by the deserted place, where only a broken thread of ice-cold water trickles its way down to the roadside, and fancy how eagerly, in the broad summer days, the horses, panting through the heavy sand and up the rocky hills, thrust their noses deep into the overflowing trough of crystal coolness, while, now and then, the cautious dri-vers pulled up their heads with a jerk, until they heard the long-drawn breath of inarticulate content.

We like to think that the dripping cup was borne to bearded lips that were eloquent and true of old, and lips, maybe, of beauty, that are dusty and dumb to-day; that bees from the shimmering fields came bugling thither, and crept, with dainty feet, along the trough's damp edge; that birds sat there, and drank and rendered their little thanks, and rode away upon the billowy air; that now and then a squirrel, red and sleek, with snowy throat, flashed chattering along the zigzag rails, and flashed away again; or a gray rabbit, with little noiseless leap and listening ears, took hurried draughts and squatted among the alders till the panting dog had lapped the nectar of the wayside spring.

There, where the Maple wears its crown, a lazy gate is swinging in the wind, sole relic of a fence that straggled round a home, of which the weedy, tangled hollow alone gives proof.

It may have been some Rachel dwelt therein, who met a second Jacob at the spring, and Fancy listens for the words they said, not found in " Ovid's Art of Love,"—the maid a matron, and the matron dead.

And then, strolling thoughtfully along, where the track grows dim, and loses itself in the grass, we come to the beeches, whereto, we like to think, glad children once made pilgrimage. That chafed and sturdy limb has borne a weight more precious than its leaves. Upon the stout old arm, swayed to and fro like canaries in a ring, swung clusters of laughing girls and boys, and then beneath it, hand-in-hand, made bows and courtesies to the passing traveler, while tattered hats of straw and wool tossed here and there proclaimed the coming stage. Ah! there *were* days when, over the old road, ran the yellow, mud-stained coach; laboring up its hills, and pitching along its log-ways, and lurching in its deep-worn tracks, and rattling down its steeps, and splashing through its brooks.

And there, in that roofless dwelling, whose clap-boards rattle in the wind, behold "the stage house" of the elder time. Very grand people used to get out of that stage sometimes, and quite as grand were the dinners that the bustling landlady and her girls set forth. Then it was that the blacksmith, in his dusty shop across the road, was wont to lean upon his hammer, and discuss the merits of wheel-horse and leader.

You can see, even to this day, the burned and blackened ring in the greensward where he used to "set the tire." Of the smithy and the man, no other trace remains.

Children sometimes wander out to the old road, and wonder where it leads, and whether to the end of the world; and we delight to join them in conjecture; to think what stalwart men they were, that, ax in hand, so bravely cut their way through the dim resounding woods, and rolled their cabins up; to think what "beauty" and what "beast" in elder times did pass along this road; what laughter echoed and what jests went round; that canvas-covered wains in many a camp were scattered towards the West, and red fires twinkled through the leafy tents; that soldiers in some old campaign, and ponderous cannon went that way to battle, and returned at last, but *fewer* than they went. This was the route of them, perhaps, who founded cities in the brave young West, its future sinews and its coming men; of newly-wedded pairs bound for the later Canaan; of murderers hastening from the hue and cry.

Across its beaten path the deer have trooped, the Indian noiseless stole, the forest shadows fallen at high noon. Westward it went to some great lake, they said, where fields all ready for the plow grew green to the water's edge, where springs came early and golden autumns lingered late.

Along that way, trampled beneath the driver's feet, the mail-bag went and came, and now and then a letter from the West; a great brown sheet, and traced with awkward pen and faded ink, yet how like a ballad ran the homely missive: of green March fields, and February flowers; of Nature's meadows waiting for the scythe; of clustering grapes that mantled all the woods; of nearest neighbors but two miles apart; of dreams of plenty and of peace. Blended therewith were memories of home and words of love sent back, and a little sigh, half breathed, for faces they never more should see.

What tidings went, sometimes, of fortunes won, and fame, by errant sons; of girls whose graves were made where the sunbeams rest, "when they promise a glorious morrow."

Thus slowly to and fro crept the sweet syllables of love, the untranslated Gospel of the human heart; and, though long on the way, they never grew chilly or old.

Ah, those letters on huge, buckram foolscap, crackling when you opened them like a fire in the hemlocks, that used to be written when letters were as honest as an open palm! Those old, half-naked letters, their blue ribs showing through, ventured out at long and painful intervals, were indited "after meeting," and were sure to contain religion, death or a wedding. The old-time writer, though wicked as Captain Kyd on week days, was bound to have religion enough in his letter to float it on Sunday, and he was no hypocrite that did it, for it was the deliberate, passionless transcript of his better self. Lay side by side an old letter of 1840 and a new letter of 1874: the one right-angled, neat and snug in its white or buff jacket, wearing a medallion as if it belonged to the legion of honor, self-folding, self-sealing, self-paying, and ready for the road. The other in its shirtsleeves, broad, long, and possibly five-cornered, written across its baggy back like a note at the bank, " for here you see the owner's name,"—an " 18¾ " or a " 25 " done in red ink in a corner, and sealed with a pat of shoe-maker's wax or a little biscuit of dough. But as honest hearts were done up in those rude letters as ever were set going, and the awkward pages were more richly illuminated than an old Saint's Legend, with unadorned and simple friendship.

But over on the new route they have strung the Telegraph, where the rise of flour and the fall of foes are transmitted by the same flash, and the price of barley and a priceless blessing go flickering along in company. The houses on the old road — what few there are left — stand with their backs to the railway and the telegraph; and the wheeled World, as it goes thundering by, looks askance upon the back-kitchens and pig-pens of the old-time.

But the houses on the new road are very new, and smell of paint; the blinds are very green, and the people very grand. The East and the West have kissed each other across the Continent, and every body and thing between is brisk as a flea, and breathless as a king's trumpeter. Even Consumption has whipped up its pale horse to a gallop, and dashed into the steeple-chase of the Age.

And year after year the old road grows dimmer, and the grass gets green across the track, and it is rechristened " the long pasture," and is surrendered to the lowing herds and the singing birds. In the midst of a region humming with life, it alone is silent, and almost awakens human sympathy, so wandering and lost and desolate it is.

Sometimes, as you dust along the turnpike, you can see it as it comes in sight round a clump of tangled trees, and " makes " as if it would venture into the new thoroughfare and go somewhere, but it never does, for, speedily sinking back into the hollow, it is lost among the willows.

Like a very old memory in the heart is it, and all forget it but the Year. Spring remembers it, and borders it with green and sprinkles it with the gold coin of the dandelion and the little stars of the Mayweed. Summer sends the bees thither to bugle among the thistle-blows, and the ground-sparrows build in its margins, and the faded ribbon of yellow sand grows bright in its glowing sun. The winds waft the breath of the morning over its desolate way, and the rains long ago beat out the old footprints it used to bear. Autumn sighs as it follows it through the ravine and among the hemlocks, and the drifts that Winter heaps are unbroken and stainless.

No bolder feet, old Road, ever left their impress on other pathways; no truer hearts than hastened on thy rugged way, have ever turned beautiful in the "better land." If there were ever those whose laugh was music, then thy woods have heard it. The daughters of the West are passing fair, but those young brows of old, whose white flashed white again from thy singing streams, and eyes glanced back to eyes —no brighter and no purer were ever bent above a classic wave.

Like thee, those brows are furrowed and those eyes are dim. Like thee, Ambition's line fades from the eye of Time, and like the dusty "runways" of thy brooks, soft pulses have grown dry and dumb.

CHAPTER VII.

A BIRD HEAVEN.

DOES any theological reason exist why there should not be in some blessed planet or other a Bird Heaven, a realm where the green gates of Spring are forever opening and the fruits of Summer are for ever ripening, whose skies are full of the downiest of clouds and the softest of songs?

Were I to be constituted the Peter of the gate of that Paradise, there are very few birds to which free entrance should not be given, except Cochin China, Shanghai, and Bramah Pootrah hens; the raven should be admitted for the sake of the poet, and even the owl should have a hollow tree all to itself, and a meadow of mice for its portion; but for prowling cats and naughty boys, for snares and for fowlers, there should be no salvation. No early frosts, no chilling rains, the cherries all free, and great fields of grain for the pigeons. Birds, everywhere birds! Not a bush but would have a song in it, all trees would be "singing trees," and all nests sacred as so many little arks of the Covenant.

Wicker baskets full of pearls with life in them, emeralds with song in them, swinging from bending bough, hidden in the grass, rocking among the rushes, like the little Moses of old, and everybody as loving as Pharaoh's daughter; no serpent in *this* Eden to charm; no sky scarred with arrows, no plumage ruffled by storm — wouldn't it be a *love* of a place, that Bird Heaven?

Just a few people that should be forever saying over to themselves, "not a sparrow falleth to the ground without Him," might live there, and the eaves, the chimneys and the peak of the barn-rafters should be full of the twitter of swallows, and the martin-box should never be untenanted. The gate-post should have a cleft for a wren to dwell in; the orchard be filled with the homes of the robin and goldfinch, and the currant-bushes thickly peopled with sparrows; nightingales should sing the night out, and the larks go heavenward to make song in the morning. The plaint of the whip-poor-will should be there, and the mourning of the wood-doves heard from the twilight of the groves. Flotillas of white sea-fowl should float upon the smooth waters, and the mote below the edge of the cloud at anchor far up in the noon, should darken into shape, for an eagle should be there in the sunshine. The old tree-trunks in the pasture should be the homestead of blue-birds all the year long, and the lilacs, like the burning bush of the mountain, should be a-blaze with the wings of red-robin and oriole, and be not consumed.

Time would forget to go on, and would tarry with June in such a midst. And the poet who so plaintively asked,

> " Where are the birds that sang
> An hundred years ago ? "

would find them there, with the sweet old song that charmed an humbler world. And, may be, we should learn the bird language then, and would know what the robins were saying, and the chirping of sparrows be turned to the choicest of English.

There in the meadow, all the days in the year, Robert o' Lincoln should ring his chime of bells; there in the leafy cloisters, " Bob White " should be incessantly called; there on the nodding thistle-blossoms, the yellow-bird should ride as the summer wind went gently by.

And what would a June be without roses? And so the sod should be enameled, and the woods should not be lonely for them. The timid children of the Rainbow, that fled before the plowshare, should grow bold again, and start up like young quails from their hiding, and cluster round the door-stone, and swing themselves up to the roof by green shrouds of their own, and swing themselves down the damp, mossy sides of the spring, and be numbered with the household.

And here, to this Bird Heaven, one should come who all his earthly life long was a loving child of Nature; who saw in the feather fallen from the blue bird in its flight the tinting of the Hand that touched the tented sky with azure; in the red bird's glowing wing, the finger-prints of Him who wove a ribbon of the falling rain, and bound therewith the cloudy brow of storm: Audubon should come and go at will. The freedom of the planet should be his.

And the world adjoining, and lying in full sight, should be a Tophet for the slayers of robins and sparrows; the men whom want of worth makes "fellows"; who lurk about the woods, in the yet unraveled leaf, and prowl in the orchards white with the sweet drift of apple-blossoms, and murder the builders of the homes of song; the ruffians who, in bright top-boots and game-bag cap-a-pie, return elated with two dead blue-birds and a lark without a head, who break a thrush's wing, and misname it "sport," and pass disguised as men. And in that Tophet they should play Nimrod, with kicking muskets shooting empty air; the crows should live with them, and Nero to fiddle for them, and a filer of saws for orchestra; and so, like Alexander the coppersmith, they should be rewarded " according to their works."

Who can imagine a birdless June, or could love a grove rich as Vallombrosa in leafy beauty, that sheltered no bird, rustled with no wings, along whose green corridors floated no little song?

With what elegance of form, grace of motion, brilliancy of coloring, and sweetness of utterance do they fill the summer world. How like carrier-doves are they, forever bringing messages of peace from the bosom of Nature even to our own; and a wintry thing indeed is the happiness that has no birds in it.

As he can not be altogether evil who cherishes a flower, makes friends with the little violet until it pleads for him, so they who love birds for their beauty and song have yet something in themselves that is lovely.

And this lingering trace of an Eden-born nature gives to the denizens of the air a commercial value beyond that of the provision market. Who would think, *without* thinking, that more than seventeen thousand song birds are annually sold in New York? The linnets, finches and thrushes of the Hartz Mountains, the canaries from Antwerp and Brussels, the skylarks from English fields, and the painted sparrows from Java are among the multitude. Seventy-five thousand dollars expended in a single city every year for birds, not to be grilled or fricasseed, but to be admired for their beauty or loved for their song! Here are the figures for a single year of this graceful trade in the city of New York:

12,500	Canaries	$31,250
600	Gold Finches	600
75	Blackbirds	525
30	Nightingales	425
600	Linnets	600
100	Skylarks	400
700	Fancy Pigeons, imported	4,000
20	Gold and Silver Pheasants	200
650	Parrots	4,900
300	Birds of Paradise	900
150	Mocking Birds	2,250
600	Java Sparrows	900
250	White and Red Cardinals	575
80	Fire Birds	225
17,000		$47,750

In 1873, ninety-five thousand canaries were sold in America — birds enough to make a golden cloud and hide the sun at high noon. And how kind it was of Chief Justice Chase to decide, in 1872, that in the intent of the law imposing a tax upon imported animals, birds were *not* ani-

mals, and so the wings and the warblers enter
the United States duty free !

Who can help following those wicker cages
with their little tenants, as, borne here and there,
they make " the winter of our discontent " a
summer ; to some gloomy room with its one window and its narrow strip of sky ; to the chamber
of the invalid and the garret of poverty. There,
under the dim sky-light, and there, by the one
window, and there, by the couch of languishing,
the captives sit and sing — sing, though no
" sweet South " is blowing, and no soft sky is
bending, and no green branch is rustling ; sit and
sing while the fall rains beat upon the panes ;
while the snows drift white upon the threshold ;
and then, when, through the smoky air and the
dull window, there comes a gush of sunshine,
what a burst of the old woodland melody there
is, till the listening heart is full of the sweet
thoughts of summer, and so they sing out sorrow's
night, and " joy cometh in the morning."

I T is with a sort of regret, shared perhaps by
nobody else, that I end these sketches. We
always get into the *habit* of things, and habit
comes to rest easily, like an old garment. I do
not now remember much of anything I was not
a little sorry to part with, except a jumping

toothache. But the best thing I can do, after
wishing my readers a pleasant trip by the World
on Wheels and a pleasant Station at last, is to

SWITCH OFF.